"**Do you always**
Stacey **asked, bit**ing her lip to curb
a smile.

"Invariably," Luc admitted straight-faced. And then he laughed. They both laughed, and what they shared in those few unguarded moments was everything she could wish for: warmth, a past that needed no explanation, and acceptance that they'd both changed and that life was better now.

"So, why aren't you in bed?" she asked cheekily as the guitarist ended one tune and segued into another.

"I should be," Luc agreed, but in a way that made her cheeks warm, and suddenly all she could think about was that thwarted kiss all those years ago. Would he push her away if she kissed him now?

"Come on—tell me—why are you here?"

"To see you," he admitted with a wicked look.

Susan Stephens was a professional singer before meeting her husband on the Mediterranean island of Malta. In true Harlequin style, they met on Monday, became engaged on Friday and married three months later. Susan enjoys entertaining, traveling and going to the theater. To relax, she reads, cooks and plays the piano, and when she's had enough of relaxing, she throws herself off mountains on skis or gallops through the countryside singing loudly.

Books by Susan Stephens

Harlequin Presents

The Sicilian's Defiant Virgin
Pregnant by the Desert King
The Greek's Virgin Temptation

One Night With Consequences

A Night of Royal Consequences
The Sheikh's Shock Child

Secret Heirs of Billionaires

The Secret Kept from the Greek

Wedlocked!

A Diamond for Del Rio's Housekeeper

Passion in Paradise

A Scandalous Midnight in Madrid

Visit the Author Profile page
at Harlequin.com for more titles.

Susan Stephens

SNOWBOUND WITH HIS FORBIDDEN INNOCENT

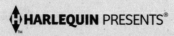

If you purchased this book without a cover you should be aware
that this book is stolen property. It was reported as "unsold and
destroyed" to the publisher, and neither the author nor the
publisher has received any payment for this "stripped book."

Recycling programs
for this product may
not exist in your area.

ISBN-13: 978-1-335-47887-0

Snowbound with His Forbidden Innocent

First North American publication 2019

Copyright © 2019 by Susan Stephens

All rights reserved. Except for use in any review, the reproduction or
utilization of this work in whole or in part in any form by any electronic,
mechanical or other means, now known or hereafter invented, including
xerography, photocopying and recording, or in any information storage
or retrieval system, is forbidden without the written permission of the
publisher, Harlequin Enterprises Limited, 22 Adelaide St. West, 40th Floor,
Toronto, Ontario M5H 4E3, Canada.

This is a work of fiction. Names, characters, places and incidents are
either the product of the author's imagination or are used fictitiously,
and any resemblance to actual persons, living or dead, business
establishments, events or locales is entirely coincidental.

This edition published by arrangement with Harlequin Books S.A.

For questions and comments about the quality of this book,
please contact us at CustomerService@Harlequin.com.

® and ™ are trademarks of Harlequin Enterprises Limited or its
corporate affiliates. Trademarks indicated with ® are registered in the
United States Patent and Trademark Office, the Canadian Intellectual
Property Office and in other countries.

Printed in U.S.A.

www.Harlequin.com

SNOWBOUND WITH
HIS FORBIDDEN
INNOCENT

For Vic, editor extraordinaire, who makes the compulsion of writing such an absolute pleasure.

CHAPTER ONE

PARTIES BORED HIM. He didn't want to go to tonight's jamboree, but his guests expected it. Ambassadors, celebrities, and royalty who craved the Da Silva glitter expected to see the head of the company and to feast at his table.

He took the short route to the ballroom via his private elevator. Senses firing on full alert, he was on his way to check every single element organised by the company he'd hired to run the event, and woe betide Party Planners if anything fell short of his expectations.

Why should it? Party Planners was reputed to be the best in the business or he wouldn't have signed off on his people hiring them. There was just one fly in that very expensive ointment. Having assumed responsibility for the event last minute when the principal of the company, Lady Sarah, had been taken ill, his best friend Niahl's kid sister, Stacey, had taken over responsibility for running his banquet in Barcelona. And, in the biggest surprise of all, his people had assured him that Stacey was now considered to be the best party planner in the business.

It was five years since he'd last seen Niahl's sister at another Party Planners event, where she hadn't exactly filled him with confidence. In fairness, she'd just started work for the company and a lot could happen in five years. On that particular occasion she'd been rushing around trying to help, spilling drinks left right and centre, in what to him, back then, had been typical Stacey. But of course his memories were of a young teenager whom he'd first met when Niahl had invited him home from university to visit their family stud farm. Niahl, Stacey and he had lived and breathed horses, and when he'd seen the quality of the animals their father was breeding, he'd determined to have his own string one day. Today he was lucky enough to be one of the foremost owners of racehorses and polo ponies in the world.

His thoughts soon strayed back to Stacey. He was curious about her, and how the change in her had occurred. She'd always tried to help, and had been slapped down for it at home, so it wasn't a surprise to him when he heard she'd gravitated towards the hospitality industry. He hoped she'd found happiness and guessed she had. She'd found none at home, where her father and his new wife had treated her like an indentured servant. No matter how hard she'd tried to please, Stacey had always been blamed, and in anyone's hearing, for the death of her mother in childbirth when she was born. No child should suffer that.

Niahl had told him that as soon as she'd been

old enough and the opportunity had presented itself, Stacey had left home. All she'd ever wanted, Niahl added, was to care for people and make them happy, no doubt in the hope that one day someone might appreciate her, as her father never had.

He shrugged as the elevator descended from the penthouse floor and his thoughts continued to run over the past five years. Stacey had obviously gone quite a way in her career, but he wondered about her personal life. He didn't want to ponder it too deeply. She'd been so fresh and innocent and he couldn't bring himself to think about her with men. He smiled, remembering her teenage crush on him. He'd never let on that he knew, but it was hard to forget that kiss in the stable when she'd lunged at him, wrapping her arms around his neck like a vice. Touching his lips where stubble was already springing sharp and black, he found the memory was as strong now as it ever had been. The yielding softness of her breasts pressing against the hard planes of his chest had never left his mind. Thinking back on it made him hard. Which was wrong. Stacey Winner was forbidden fruit. Too young, too gauche, too close to home, and a royal argumentative pain in the ass.

Stacey was the reason he'd visited the farm. Supposedly he'd been there to look at the horses he'd longed to buy one day when he'd made some money, but once he'd met her he hadn't been able to stay away. She'd kept throwing down the gauntlet, and he'd kept picking it up. She'd invigorated him, kept him alive, when the grief that had threatened to overwhelm him had become unbearable. He'd never shared his feelings with her—never shared his feelings with anyone. Nobody had suspected the battle going on inside Lucas except perhaps for Niahl, but Niahl was a good friend whereas Stacey had just liked to torment him.

He wasn't short of cash now, and could buy all the horses he liked. Some had come from their farm— whatever else he was, Stacey's father knew his horseflesh—and had gone on to become winners, or to earn fortunes at stud. The tech company Luc had founded in his bedroom as a desperate measure to pay off his parents' debts went from strength to strength. Money kept pouring in. He couldn't stop it if he tried.

Determined to support his siblings when their parents had been killed in a tragic accident and the bank had called in his parents' loans, he'd used an ancient computer to put together a program that traced bloodlines of horses across the world. One programme had led to another until Da Silva Inc had offices in every major capital, but his first love remained horses and the wild foothills of the Sierra Nevada where the animals thrived on his *estancia*.

As the elevator slowed to a halt, and the steel door slid open with a muted hiss, he stepped out on the ballroom level. He couldn't help but be aware of the interest he provoked. Da Silva Inc was now a top company. Thanks to his talent for tech, and with desperation driving him forwards, he was the owner of all he surveyed, including this hotel. But it was not his natural habitat. Staring at the glittering scene beyond the grand double doors leading into the ballroom, he wished he were riding the trail, but this lavish banquet was an opportunity for him to thank his staff, and to raise money from the great and good for an array of well-deserving charities. No matter that he was already uncomfortable in his custom-made suit, with the stiff white collar of his shirt cutting into his neck and the black tie he'd fastened while snarling into the mirror strangling him, he would move heaven and earth to make tonight a success. Untying the bow tie, he opened the top button of his shirt and cracked his neck with pleasure. There had to be some compensations for running the show, though he longed for the freedom of the trail and a flat-out gallop.

He scanned the bustling space, but while his eyes clocked mundane details, his mind was fixed on finding Stacey. What differences would five years have made? His people had dealt with the minutiae of the contract and briefing meetings so there'd been no reason for him to get involved. He hoped she was happy. She was certainly successful. But how would she behave towards him? Would she be reserved now she was older and presumably wiser, or would that demon glint still flare in her eyes? Part of him hoped for the latter, but his guests deserved a calm, well-run evening with no drama to ruffle their expensive feathers. He'd called her room, but there'd been no answer. The party was almost due to begin. She should be here… So where was she?

He quartered the ballroom, pacing like a hunting wolf with its senses raw and flaring. Guests were starting to arrive. Curious glances came his way. Some women took an involuntary step back, fearing his reputation, while others, attracted to danger, gave him signals as old as time. They meant nothing to him. His only ambition had ever been to blank his mind to the horror of his parents' death, and then to care for his siblings. He had no time for romance, and no need of it, either. His business had brought him wealth beyond imagining, which made any and all distractions available, though horses remained the love of his life. A string of high-profile, though ultimately meaningless, affairs were useful in that they allowed him not to dwell too deeply on himself.

As he passed the bar he remembered the last time he and Stacey had met. She'd knocked a drink over his companion by accident, costing him a replacement couture gown. He hadn't troubled her with the detail, as Stacey had very kindly offered to have the dress cleaned. Naturally that hadn't suited the woman on his arm at the time, who had seen the incident as an opportunity to add to her greedy haul. It had certainly proved a necessary wake-up call for him. He'd arranged for his PA to deliver the usual pay-off to the woman in the form of an expensive jewel, delivered the next morning, together with a new, far more expensive dress.

Why had fate chosen to put Stacey in his way again?

Or had he put her in his way? His people worked

on the finer details of an event, but it was up to him
to okay the contract. With a short cynical laugh, he
acknowledged that he missed their verbal jousting.
No one stood up to him as Stacey did, and he was
weary of being fawned over. He craved her stimu-
lating presence, even though she used to drive him
crazy with the tricks she played on him at the farm.
He missed the looks that passed between them and
the electricity that sparked whenever they were close.
It was ironic that a man who could buy anything
couldn't buy the one thing he wanted: a few moments of her time.

Money meant nothing to Stacey. She'd proved that
on the day he'd bought her favourite horse. He hadn't
realised when her father had offered him the promising colt that the animal had meant so much to Stacey. When transport had arrived to take the horse to
his *estancia* in Spain, he'd offered Stacey the same
money he'd paid her father if she would just stop
crying. He couldn't have said anything to annoy her
more, and she'd flung everything she could get her
hands on at him. It had done him no good at all to
point out that the money would pay her college fees.

'I hate you!' she'd screamed. 'You don't know
anything about love. All you care about is money!'
That had hurt because he did know about love. The
pain of losing his parents never left him, though he
rarely examined that grief, knowing it might swamp
him if he did. 'If you hurt Ludo, I'll kill you!' she'd
vowed. Staring into Stacey's wounded green eyes,
he'd understood the anguish of someone who relied

on a madcap brother and a horse for affection; she was losing one of them, when she couldn't afford to lose either.

'Is everything to your satisfaction, Señor Da Silva?'

He swung around to find the hotel manager hovering anxiously behind him. Such was the power Da Silva Inc wielded that however he tried to make things easy for people they literally trembled at the thought of letting him down.

'If anything falls short in your eyes, Señor Da Silva—' the manager wrung his hands at the thought '—my staff will quickly make it right for you, though I have to say Party Planners has excelled itself. I can't remember any big event we've held here running quite so smoothly.'

'Thank you for the reassurance, *señor*,' Lucas returned politely. 'I was just thinking the same thing.' As there was still no sign of Stacey, he asked, 'The team leader of Party Planners—have you seen her?'

'Ah, yes, *señor*. Señorita Winner is in the kitchen checking last-minute details.'

The manager looked relieved that he had finally been of help, and Lucas gave his arm a reassuring pat. 'You and your staff are top class, and I know you will give the party planners every assistance.'

Why hadn't she come to find him? He ground his jaw as the manager hurried away. Surely the client was important too?

So thinks a man who hasn't given Stacey's whereabouts or well-being a passing thought for the past five years, he mused. *And yet now I expect her to dance attendance on me?*

Frankly, yes. Da Silva Inc was everyone's most valuable account. To be associated with his company was considered a seal of quality, as well as a guarantee of future success. She should be thanking him, not avoiding him.

Was that his problem? Or was it picturing Stacey as she might be now, a worldly and experienced woman, socially and sexually confident in any setting?

That might be grating on his tetchy psyche, he conceded grudgingly. She'd always had her own mind, and would no doubt appear when she was ready, and not a moment before. And if he didn't know what to expect, at least he knew what he wanted.

He wanted the wild child Stacey had been as a teenager, the woman who could be infuriating one minute and then caring and tender the next. He wanted all of her and he wanted her now, for, as frustratingly defiant as Stacey was, she could light up a room. Every other woman present would fall short because of her.

Irritating, impossible to ignore, beautiful, *vulnerable* Stacey...

And that vulnerability was the very reason he couldn't have her. She'd been through enough. He was no saint. No comfort blanket, either. He was a hard-bitten businessman with ice where his heart used to live, who only cared for his siblings, his staff, and the charities he supported. Beyond that was a vast, uncharted region he had no intention of exploring.

By the time he reached the kitchen he had convinced himself that it would be better if he didn't see Stacey. There'd be no chance to stand and chat, and a man of his appetite shouldn't contemplate toying with the sister of his friend. Instead, he sought distraction in the winter wonderland she had created in the ballroom. A champagne fountain, its glasses seemingly precariously balanced, reached all the way to the mezzanine floor. Ice carvers were putting the finishing touches to their life-sized sculptures of horses and riders, while in another corner there was an ice bar—which perfectly suited his mood— where cocktail waiters defied gravity as they practised tossing their bottles about. Turning, he viewed the circular dance floor around which tables were dressed for a lavish banquet. The best chefs in the world would cook for his guests, and had competed for the honour of being chosen for this privilege. Heavy carved crystal glasses sat atop crisp white linen waiting to be filled with vintage wines and champagne, while a forest of candles lit the scene. His chosen colour scheme of green and white had been executed to perfection. The floral displays were both extravagant and stylish. Wait staff had assembled, and the orchestra was tuning up. An excited tension filled the ballroom, promising a night to remember.

Like a finely bred horse held on a short rein, everything around him was on the point of leaping into action. Except his libido, he conceded with a twist of his lips, which he would stamp on tonight.

Everything was on the point of being ready. Stacey loved this moment just before the starting gun went off. She was still dressed in jeans and a tee shirt, ready to help out wherever she could, but she wanted to be showered and dressed as elegantly as she could to witness the excitement of the guests when they saw the room for the first time, and feel the tension of the hard-working chefs and staff as they waited for service to begin. She found this early atmosphere at any event infectious. It always sent a frisson of anticipation rippling down her spine, though tonight that frisson was more of an earthquake at the thought of seeing Lucas again. She couldn't wait to prove herself, and show what the team could do. She wanted him to know that she'd made it—perhaps not to his level in the financial sense, but she could *do* this and, more importantly, she loved doing this. What the Da Silva people couldn't know was that Lady Sarah, the owner of Party Planners, had been taken ill and the bank was threatening to foreclose, but if Stacey could keep things on an even keel tonight, and secure the next contract with Da Silva, the bank had promised to back off. They wouldn't lose the Da Silva account, of that she was grimly determined. The team had worked too hard. If anything did go wrong, she would take responsibility.

Coming face to face with the man who'd given

her so many sleepless nights when she was a teen-ager was something else. It should have been easy, as she'd kept track of Lucas through Niahl and through the press. Lucas was frequently pictured with this princess or that celebrity, always looking glorious but elegantly bored. He'd never had much time for glitz, she remembered. Would he be with someone tonight? She tensed at the thought.

She couldn't bear it.

She had to bear it.

Lucas didn't belong to her and never had. He was her brother's friend, and he and Niahl moved in very different circles. Stacey had always been happiest on the ground floor, grafting alongside her co-workers, while Lucas preferred an ivory tower—just so long as there was a stable close by.

Spirits were high when the Party Planners team assembled for a last-minute briefing in the office adjacent to the ballroom. This was a glamorous and exciting occasion, and, even in a packed diary of similar glamorous and exciting occasions, the Da Silva party stood out, mainly because the owner and founder of the company was in the building. There wasn't a single member of the team who hadn't heard about Lucas Da Silva, or wondered what he was like in person. His prowess in business was common knowledge, as was his blistering talent on the polo field, together with his uncanny ability to train and bring on winning racehorses. Everyone was buzzing at the thought of seeing him, even from a distance, and that included Stacey.

Would she stand up to him as she had in the past? Would she toss a drink over his date if he had one? *Resist! That's just nerves talking.*

Or would their client relationship get in the way of all that? The only thing that mattered, she reminded herself firmly, was proving to Lucas that she and the team were the best people for this job.

Her first sight of Lucas Da Silva sucked the air from her lungs. At least he was alone, with no companion in sight. *Yet.* Whatever she'd been expecting, pictured or imagined, nothing came close to how Luc looked now. Hot back in the day in breeches or a pair of old jeans he was unbelievably attractive in a formal dinner suit. And five years had done him favours. Taller than average, he was even more compelling. Age had added gravitas to his quiver of assets. Dressed impeccably with black diamonds glittering at his cuffs, he'd left one button open on his shirt and wore his bow tie slung around his neck. Only Lucas, she mused with a short, rueful laugh. Built like a gladiator, with shoulders wide enough to hoist an ox, he exuded the type of dangerous glamour that had every woman present attempting to attract his attention. With the exception of Stacey, for whom familiarity had bred frustrated acceptance that Lucas probably still thought of her as the annoying younger sister of his friend.

She recognised the expression of tolerance mixed with tamped-down fire on his face, and knew what had caused it. Lucas was happiest mounted on the strongest stallion, testing the animal, testing himself. This easy life of unsurpassed luxury and entitlement was not for him, not really—he paid lip service to the world into which his tech savvy had launched him. Having said that, he'd look amazing no matter whether his bow tie was neatly tied or hanging loose—probably best wearing nothing at all, though she would be wise not to allow her thoughts to stray in that direction. It was enough to say the pictures in magazines didn't come close to doing him justice. Power emanated from him. As she watched him work the room, she could imagine sparks of testosterone firing off him like rockets on the fourth of July.

Yes, he was formidable, but she had a job to do. She would welcome him to the event, and be ready to take any criticism he might care to offer, and then act on it immediately. She had to secure that next contract. The annual Da Silva event in the mountains was even bigger than this banquet but when news leaked, as it surely would, that Lady Sarah was ill, would Lucas trust Stacey to take her place?

He had to. She'd make sure of it any way she could.

As the team left to complete their various tasks, Stacey had a moment to think. Her thoughts turned to the man her gaze was following around the ballroom. Forget five years ago when she'd been a blundering intern, trying her best and achieving her worst by spilling a drink down his date, all she could think about was that kiss…that *almost* kiss, when her feelings had triumphed over her rational mind. Teenage hormones had played a part, but that couldn't be the whole story or why would she feel now that if she had Lucas boxed in a corner she'd do exactly the same thing? She was a woman, not a flush-faced teen, and she had appetites like everyone else.

She broke off there to go and check that there was enough champagne on ice, with more crates waiting to fill the spaces in the chiller as soon as the first batch had left for the tables. It was inevitable as she worked that she thought about Lucas. He'd been there the day she'd decided to leave home, and had played a large part in her decision. She'd felt very differently about him on that occasion, and tightened her mouth now at the memory. He'd found her in the stable saying goodbye to the colt she'd cared for all its lively, spirited, magical life. She could even remember looking around, heart racing, thinking Lucas had come to tell her that he'd changed his mind and that she could keep Ludo, but instead he'd offered her money. What had hurt even more was that he'd understood so little about her. If he'd thought cold cash could replace a beloved animal, he hadn't known her at all. Her father had promised he would never sell Ludo. They'd breed from him, he'd said. But he'd lied.

She'd learned later that Lucas hadn't realised Ludo was her horse when he'd made the offer, but her father had sold him on without even telling her. That had been the straw that broke the camel's back. She'd been thinking about leaving the restrictions of the farm, and after that there had been no reason to stay. The only way she could ever keep an animal was by funding it herself, and to do that she had to study and gain qualifications. A career was the only route to independence.

She gave those members of the team dealing with the supply of drinks the go-ahead to stack the extra cases of champagne out of the way but close by the chiller ready to reload, and joined them in moving the heavy boxes. Lucas wasn't to blame for her decision to leave home, she reflected as she got into the rhythm of lift, carry and lower. Actually, she should thank him. This was a great job, and she had fantastic co-workers. Even out of sight of the ballroom the atmosphere was upbeat and positive.

What a contrast to life on the farm, she reflected as she gave everyone their official half-hour notice to the doors opening to the Da Silva guests. Everyone here supported each other and remained upbeat. Whatever challenges they might face, they faced together. She was happy here amongst friends. Her father had never liked her, and his new wife liked Stacey even less. With Ludo gone there had been no reason not to leave the isolated farm. It had been a chance to test herself in the big city, and now she was a professional woman with a job to do, Stacey reminded herself as she hurried back to the ballroom on another mission. She'd do everything she could to keep Lucas happy tonight and Party Planners in business. She'd prove herself to him, in the business sense, that was—not that Lucas had ever shown the slightest interest in any other kind of relationship with her, she reflected wryly.

She was halfway across the dance floor when a member of the team stopped her to say that some of the guests were swapping around the place cards on the tables so they could sit closer to Señor Da Silva.

'Right,' Stacey said, firming her jaw. 'Leave this to me.' They'd spent hours on the seating plan. A strict order of hierarchy had to be observed at these events, as it was all too easy to cause offence. Her guess was that Lucas wouldn't care where he sat, but his guests would.

By the time she had set things to rights there was no sign of him. Her stomach clenched with tension, requiring her to silently reinforce the message that when they met she would assume her customary cool, professional persona. It was important to keep on his right side to make sure he didn't pull the next contract.

Which didn't mean the right side of his bed, she informed her disappointed body firmly.

CHAPTER TWO

HE BROODED WITH irritation as he caught sight of
Stacey hurrying around the ballroom without once
glancing his way. Dressed casually, with no make-
up on her face and her hair scraped back, she still
looked punch-in-the-gut beautiful to him. The run-
up to any event was hectic, but that didn't excuse
her not seeking him out. *Am I the client, or am I
not?*

*She's busy. Isn't that what you want and expect
of a party planner in the hour before your guests
arrive?*

He drew a steadying breath. For once in his
charmed life what he wanted and what he could
have were facing each other across a great divide.
He shrugged. So he'd close that gap.

At last she was back in her room, safe in the knowledge that she and the team had every aspect of the
night ahead covered between them. With very little
time to review her choice of gown it was lucky she'd
made her decision earlier. Seeing Lucas again had

shaken her to the core. When he wasn't in her life she thought about him constantly, and now he was here, a real physical presence in this same building, she couldn't think of anything else, and she had to, she *must*. The *only* thing she must think about to-night was the work she loved.

Closing her eyes, she blew out a shaky breath. She had a phone call to make, and needed her wits about her to do that. Since Lady Sarah had put her in charge of running the Da Silva account, Stacey had established an excellent working relationship with the top people at Da Silva and wanted to give them a heads-up to make sure she wasn't treading on any toes when she told Lucas she'd also be running his party in the mountains. It was no use burying her head in the sand. He had to know, and she had to be the one to tell him, and the sooner the better.

Her counterpart greeted her warmly, and listened carefully before admitting that, just as Stacey had suspected, they'd seen no reason to trouble Lucas with the fact that Stacey was in charge of his big an-nual event in the mountains. Lady Sarah's word was good enough for them. 'We haven't kept it a secret,' the woman explained. 'He doesn't appreciate gossip, and expects us to get on with things, so there was no reason to trouble him with the fact that Lady Sarah is unwell, and you're taking over.'

'That's what I thought,' Stacey admitted. 'Don't worry. I'll handle it.'

'No other problems?'

'None,' she confirmed, wishing that were true. She could pretend to other people, but not to herself, and Lucas coming back into her world had changed everything.

The outfit she'd put together was stylish enough to blend into the sophisticated crowd, yet discreet, so it wouldn't clash in colour or style with anything one of the high-profile guests might choose to wear. A limited budget had confined her choices to the high street, but she'd been lucky enough to find some great buys on the sale rails of a famous store, including this simple column of lightweight cream silk. Ankle length, the gown reached just above the nude pumps she'd chosen to take her through the night, knowing she'd be on her feet for most if not all of the evening. The neckline was discreet, and boasted a collar and lapel that gave the elegant sheath a passing nod to a business suit. Having tamed her wild red curls into a simple updo, she tucked a slim radio into her understated evening clutch, swung a lanyard around her neck to make sure she was easily identifiable, and, having checked her lip gloss, she spritzed on some scent and headed out.

She checked her watch as she stepped into the elevator. Perfect timing. Her heart was racing—and not just with excitement at the thought of the impending party. Would Lucas feel anything when he saw her? No, she concluded with a wry, accepting curve of her mouth. He'd be as smoulderingly unconcerned as ever. But that didn't stop her pulse spiking at the thought of seeing him again.

* * *

His first meet with Stacey did not go as he had expected. He cut her off in the ballroom, where, typically, she was rushing about.

'I'm sorry, Lucas, but I can't stop to talk now—'

'I beg your pardon?' He jerked his head back with surprise. 'Is that all I get?'

She stood poised for flight. 'After five long years?' she suggested, her eyes searching his. Professional or not, she'd always been a participant, never afraid to take on a challenge, rather than a person content to laze on the benches. He took some consolation from the fact that those beautiful green eyes had darkened, and her breath was both audible and fast. 'Are you run off your feet?' he suggested dryly as she snatched a breath.

She was smart and knew at once what he meant. 'I'm quite calm,' she assured him with the lift of one elegant brow, as if to say, *You don't faze me*, and swiftly following on with, *Not everyone falls at your feet*. Then professionalism kicked in. Fully aware that she was speaking to a client, she hit him with an old memory. 'You don't need to worry about drinks going flying tonight.'

'Do I need to worry about anything else?' he queried, staring down into her crystal-clear gaze.

She held her breath and then released it. 'No,' she said with confidence. 'Good to see you, Lucas,' she added as a prelude to dashing off. 'You look well.'

'You look flushed.'

'The heat in here—'

He pinned a frown to his face. 'If the air con isn't up to the job—'

'It is,' she flashed.

'Then…?'

'Then, I have to get on.'

He smiled faintly. 'Don't let me stop you…'

'You won't,' she assured him, and was he imagining it, or were her shoulders tense with awareness as she hurried away?

A member of staff attracted her attention and Stacey moved on to sort out another problem, leaving him in the unusual position of standing watching the action, rather than directing it. And he wanted more. A lot more. Those scant few minutes hadn't been enough. Had they been enough for Stacey? Her eyes suggested not, but dedication to her job clearly overruled her personal feelings, leaving him more frustrated than he could remember. Did she feel the same? She didn't glance back once.

She couldn't just walk away.

But she had.

The last time he'd looked in the mirror Lucas Da Silva had stared back. *He* was supposed to give the rain check, not Stacey. He huffed with grim amusement. She clearly hadn't read the rulebook. That must have gone out of the window when she left the farm—not that she'd been easy then. Stacey Winner had always been a piece of work. And looked amazing, he conceded as he followed her progress around the ballroom, trying not to think of her moaning in his arms and begging for more. Her carefully ar-

ranged hair was still damp from the shower and her
make-up was simple, but she'd undergone a complete transformation from casual tee shirt and jeans
into an elegant, ankle-length gown of cream silk that
moulded her lush form with loving attention to detail. He watched as she stopped to reassure a member
of staff with her arm around the woman's shoulders.
As soon as the team member returned to her duties
he made his move. There was no reason why Stacey
couldn't speak to him now.

She had survived the first encounter with Lucas.
Doing a little happy dance inside, she was a little
breathless and a lot shaken up, but...*I survived!* And
felt a little proud at the thought that she had managed to revive the old banter they used to share on
the farm, yet had maintained a reasonable balance
between her personal and her professional persona.
At least, she hoped she had, Stacey reflected as she
glanced across at Lucas, who was speaking to members of the band. Seeing him from a distance like this
was bad enough, she mused, moving on. Standing
close enough to touch him was a torment with no
parole. He was like a force field, threatening to suck
her in and turn her brain to jelly and she couldn't afford to have that happen tonight.

'Stacey.'

'Lucas!'

He was right behind her. And it happened again.
Her brain turned to mush, while her feet appeared
to be welded to the spot. Forcing herself into a pro-

fessional frame of mind, she focused on the job in hand. 'The doors will open in a few minutes,' she exclaimed brightly as he opened his mouth to say something, and then she slipped away.

Cursing beneath his breath, he determined they would spend time together. Admittedly that was difficult for her now, but it wouldn't always be so.

He was too used to everything being easy, he supposed, to women staring at him with lust in their eyes and dollar signs. Stacey was different. She was a novelty. *Novelty was the most valuable possession a wealthy man could have.*

Hard luck, he reflected with grim amusement. As far as he could tell, there was nothing in Stacey's expression but passion for her work, and determination to make tonight a success.

Left to stand and stare as she moved around the glittering ballroom like a rather glamorous automaton on wheels, he ground his jaw and, with an exclamation born of pure frustration, he left to take up his role as host. Seeing Stacey again had roused feelings inside him he wouldn't have believed himself capable of, and there was only one thing to cure that. And then she turned to stare at him, still with no hint of lust or dollar signs in her eyes, but instead they seemed to say, 'What do you think of this fabulous setting? Hasn't the team worked hard?'

Infuriating woman. This wasn't the farm, and she was no longer the teenager playing tricks on her brother's friend. Had she forgotten that he was the client, and it was he who was paying the bill? Then, right out of the blue, there it was, the flash of mischief in her eyes, the demon glint he remembered. Shaking his head, he returned that look with a dark, warning glance, but his irritation had melted away.

She rewarded him with a smile so engaging he wanted to have her on the spot. His timing was definitely out. The grand double doors had just opened and his guests were pouring in. Forced to banish his physical reaction to Stacey by sheer force of will, he gave himself a sharp reminder that she had never been in awe of him. He could stand on his dignity as much as he liked and all she would do was smile back.

From the first time Niahl had brought him home to trial the ponies on the farm, Stacey had tested him. Daring him to ride their wildest horse, she would jump down from the fence where she was perched, seemingly uninterested, and walk away when the animal responded to his firm, yet sympathetic hand. She was fearless on horseback, and had often attempted to outride him. 'Anything's possible,' she'd tell him stubbornly as she trotted into the yard after him. 'I'll get you next time.' She never gave up, and became increasingly ingenious when it came to stopping him buying her favourite ponies. 'You'll be far too demanding,' she'd say, blushing because she knew this was a lie. 'You'll break their spirit.' The ponies in question, according to Stacey, were variously winded or lame, and would almost certainly disappoint him in every way. These supposed facts she would state with her big green eyes wide open, and as soon as she got the chance she'd free the animals from their stable and shoo them into the wild, forcing him and her brother to round them up again. Everyone but him had been surprised when she left home. He suspected her father had been relieved. His new wife had made no secret of her relief. She'd never liked Stacey. Perhaps only Lucas and Niahl had appreciated the courage it had taken for Stacey to seek out a new life in the big city when she'd barely travelled more than five miles from the farm.

She'd always loved a challenge. So did he, he reflected as he watched Stacey greet the first of his guests. He leaned back against the wall as she guided the various luminaries to their places. She did this with charm and grace, making his high-tone guests look clumsy. Stacey Winner was as intriguing as the wild ponies he loved to ride. It didn't hurt that she looked fabulous tonight. Simplicity was everything in his eyes. True glamour meant appreciating what nature had bestowed and making the most of it, and she'd done this to perfection. Compared to Stacey, every woman in the place appeared contrived, overdressed, shrill. They failed to hold his attention, while Stacey, with her gleaming hair and can-do attitude, was everything he'd been waiting for.

And couldn't have, he reminded himself as his tightening groin ached a warning. Stacey Winner was forbidden fruit. His life was fast-moving with no room for passengers. She was Niahl's beloved kid

sister, and he had no intention of risking his friendship with Niahl.

As if she knew the path his thoughts were taking, Stacey glanced his way, then swung away fast.
Was she blushing? Did he affect her as she affected
him? Should he care? Only one thing was certain:
beneath the professional shell she had developed over
the past five years, the same fire burned. She was
just better at hiding it.

But uncovering that passion and watching it break
free was a pleasure he would never know.

While he'd been studying Stacey, the ballroom
had filled up. The smiles on the faces of his guests
confirmed what he already knew. Party Planners had
done a great job. He returned Stacey's glance with a
shrug and a stare full of irony that said, *Well done.*

Watch me, the demon glint insisted. *I'm not done
yet.*

Oh, he would. How could he not, when the gown
she was wearing displayed every luscious curve, and
though her flamboyant red hair had been tamed for
the evening it wouldn't take much to pull out those
pins to fist a hank and kiss her neck? The hairstyle
flaunted cheekbones he hadn't even realised existed.
Maybe they hadn't existed five years ago. *Maybe
a lot of things had changed in five years.* He felt
a spear of jealousy to think of some man—maybe
men—touching her. Which was ridiculous when she
would never be his.

Smoothing his hackles back down again, he continued his inspection. It was Stacey's quiet confi-

dence that impressed him the most, he decided. That and the glaringly obvious—that she was classy and stylish with a particular brand of humour that appealed to him.

Avoiding close contact with Stacey was a must, he accepted with a grim twist to his mouth. His party in the mountains was a no-go if he wanted to keep things platonic between them. He was a man, not a saint.

A fact that was proved the very next moment when he noticed an elderly ambassador place his wizened paw on Stacey's back. The urge to knock him away was overwhelming, which was ridiculous. He was more in control than that, surely?

Apparently not, he accepted as he strode across the ballroom? *She was his.* To protect, he amended swiftly, as he would protect any woman in the same situation.

By the time he reached Stacey, she had skilfully evaded the aging satyr and moved on, but no sooner had she extricated herself from one difficult situation than she was confronted by another in the form of a notoriously difficult film star. The prima donna had already laid waste to several junior members of the Party Planners team by the time Stacey reached the tense group. With a quick kind word to her co-workers, she took over, making it clear that anything the woman wanted would be provided. The diva was already seated in the prized central spot where everyone could see and admire her, but there appeared to be something on the table that displeased her. Curious as to what this might be, he drew closer.

'Remove that disgusting greenery,' the woman instructed. 'My people should have informed you that I'm allergic to foliage, and only white roses are acceptable on my table.'

Where exactly would she get white roses at this late stage? he wondered as Stacey soothed the woman, while discreetly giving instructions to a member of her team. Clearly determined to keep everything under control and to protect his other guests, she showed a steely front as she moved quickly into action.

'Nothing is too much trouble for a VIP everyone is honoured to welcome,' she assured the star. 'I will personally ensure that this unfortunate error is put right immediately. In the meantime,' she added, calling a waiter, 'a magnum of vintage champagne for our guest. And perhaps you would like to meet Prince Albert of Villebourg sur Mer?' she suggested to the now somewhat mollified celebrity.

As the diva's eyes gleamed, he thought, *Bravo, Stacey*. And *bravo* a second time, he concluded wryly as an assistant hurried into the ballroom with a florist in tow. Stacey had not only arranged an exclusive photo shoot with the prince for her difficult guest, but had arranged for the orchestra to play the theme tune from the diva's latest film, and while this was happening the original centrepiece was being replaced by one composed entirely of white roses.

A triumph, Señorita Winner! He was pleased for

her. But—was he imagining it or had Stacey just stared at him with a 'Now what have you got to say for yourself?' smile? Whatever he thought he knew about Stacey, he realised he had a lot to learn, and she had made him impatient to fill in the gaps.

There would always be hitches, Stacey accepted as she continued with her duties. Solving those hitches was half the fun of the job. It pleased her to find answers, and to make people happy. And not just because Señor Iron Britches was in the room, though Luc rocked her world and made her body yearn each time their stares clashed. Formal wear suited him. Emphasising his height and the width of his shoulders, it gilded the darkly glittering glamour he was famous for. Though Luc looked just as good in a pair of banged-up jeans…or those shots of him in polo magazines wearing tight-fitting breeches… Better not think about tight-fitting breeches, or she wouldn't get any work done. She had better things to do than admire a client's butt.

In her defence, not every client had a butt like Lucas Da Silva.

CHAPTER THREE

SHE WASN'T GETTING away from him this time. He stepped in front of Stacey the first time their paths crossed. 'Señorita Winner, I'm beginning to think you're avoiding me.'

She looked at him wide-eyed. 'Why would I do that?'

Her manner was as direct as ever, and held nothing more than professional interest. Opening her arms wide, she explained, 'Forgive me. We've been very busy tonight, but I hope you're pleased with what we've achieved so far?'

'I am pleased,' he admitted. 'You've dealt with some difficult guests, defusing situations that could have disrupted other people's enjoyment of the evening.'

Stacey shrugged. 'I want everyone to enjoy themselves whoever they are. We all have different expectations.'

'Indeed,' he agreed, staring deep into her eyes.

She searched his as if expecting to find mockery there, and, finding none, she smiled. 'Anyway, thank you for the compliment. I'll accept it on behalf of the team. But now, if you'll excuse me, I have one more thing to check before the banquet begins.'

'Which is?' he queried.

'I want to make sure that no one else has swapped around their place card to sit closer to you.'

He laughed. 'Am I so much in demand?'

'You know you are,' she said with one of her classic withering looks.

'But not with you, I take it?'

'I don't know what you mean,' she said, but she couldn't meet his eyes.

'Forget it.' He made her a mock bow. 'And thank you for protecting me.'

'My pleasure,' she assured him, on the point of hurrying away.

'So, where *am* I sitting?' he asked to keep her close a little longer.

'Next to me.' She held his surprised stare in an amused look of her own. 'I thought you'd like that. You don't have a companion tonight, and I've seated the princess on your other side. I'll be on hand to run errands.'

'You? Run errands?' he queried suspiciously.

'Yes. Like a PA, or an assistant,' she said in a matter-of-fact tone.

'And you don't mind that?'

'Why should I? I'm here to work. If you'd rather I sat somewhere else—'

'No,' he said so fast he startled both of them. 'I'm happy with the arrangements as they are.'

'Then…' She looked at him questioningly. 'If you'll excuse me?'

'Of course,' he said with a slight dip of his head. 'Don't let me keep you.'

She didn't see Lucas again until everyone was seated for the banquet and she finally took her place beside him. 'I was only joking about sitting down,' she explained as a waiter settled a napkin on her lap with a flourish. 'I wasn't sure if you had someone in mind to take this place, and now I don't want to leave an empty seat beside you.'

'That wouldn't look good,' Luc agreed. 'Is that the only reason you came to sit next to me?' He gave her a long, sideways look.

'I can't think of any other reason,' she said, though she knew she had to broach the subject of Lady Sarah's leave of absence.

'You impressed me tonight.'

'You mean the team impressed you tonight,' she prompted.

'I mean you.'

Luc's tone was soft and husky and he held her gaze several beats too long. She took advantage of the moment to ask him, 'Does that mean the next contract's secure?'

He frowned. 'Is there something you'd like to tell me?'

He'd already heard, she guessed. Lucas hadn't climbed the greasy pole of success without doing his research. She guessed he'd brought up her CV to check on her rise through the company, and would know the latest news on Party Planners, including the fact that Lady Sarah was ill. If she knew anything at all about Lucas Da Silva, she was prepared to bet he was on the case. 'Only that Lady Sarah is unwell and has asked me to run this function as well as the next for you. Do you have a problem with that?'

'A problem?' Luc dipped his chin to fix her with a questioning stare.

'The team has turned itself inside out for you, and will happily do so again.'

'And I will thank them,' he said.

'But?'

'You want assurances here and now?'

Before she could answer, a member of her team made a discreet gesture that would take Stacey away from the table. 'If you'll excuse me, I have to go.'

'You're not even going to stay long enough to test the food?'

'I trust your chefs.'

'That's very good of you,' Lucas commented dryly.

'I trust you,' she said, touching his arm to drive the point home.

Immediately, she wished she hadn't done that. It was as if she'd plugged her hand into an electric socket. Her fingers were actually tingling. What she should be asking herself was whether Lucas would trust her enough to let her run an event as important to his company as the annual escape to the mountains. To make matters worse, it now seemed their old connection was as strong as ever, and she couldn't resist teasing him before leaving the table. 'Would you like me to deliver the happy news to one of the placecard-swapping starlets that a seat has become available next to their host?'

'You'll do no such—!'

Damn the woman! She'd gone! And with a smile on her mouth that promised she could still give as good as she got. This was like being back on the farm, where for every trick Stacey played on him he paid her back. His hackles were bristling. And his groin was in torment. He huffed a humourless laugh. Perhaps he deserved this, deserved the demon glint in her eyes, deserved Stacey.

He was still mulling this over when a young woman he vaguely recognised from the polo circuit approached the empty seat next to him, and, with what she must have imagined was a winsome expression on her avaricious face, commented, 'You look lonely.'

'Do I?' Standing as good manners demanded, he waited until she'd sat down and he'd introduced her to a handsome young diplomat in the next chair. 'I was distracted,' he explained, swiping a hand across his forehead. 'And unfortunately, I've just been called away. Please forgive me.' He summoned a waiter. 'Champagne for my guests.'

He left the table with relief. Whatever kind of spin he'd put on saving Stacey from the excesses playing on a loop in his mind had evaporated. They couldn't leave things here. Confrontation between them was

a given. Why try to avoid it? He knew when to pull
back, didn't he? Maybe not, he reflected as he crossed
the dance floor in search of the one woman he would
consider dancing with tonight. His primal self had
roared to the surface of his outwardly civilised ve-
neer, and it wouldn't take much to tip that over into
passion. Stacey had given him more than enough reason. He wouldn't sleep until they'd had it out.

Lucas had left the table. There was no sign of him.
Had she offended him, thereby ruining Party Planners' chances of securing the next contract? She
would never forgive herself if that were the case.
The couples on the dance floor were thinning out,
but it would be a long time until she was off duty,
because Stacey would stay until the last member of
staff had left. There were always stragglers amongst
the guests who couldn't take the hint that the people
who had worked so hard to give them a wonderful
time would like to go home at some point. The band
had been hired to play for as long as people wanted
to dance and, while both wait staff and musicians
looked exhausted, none of the guests had taken the
hint. There was only one thing for it. Politely and
firmly, she told those who seemed hardly to know
where they were any longer that the next shift would
soon be arriving to set up for breakfast, and that
the cleaners needed to come in first, and then she
stood by ready to shepherd every last partygoer out
of the room.

That done, she returned. She'd helped to tidy up

the kitchen, and now she made herself useful by checking beneath tables for forgotten items. A surprising number of things were left behind at well-lubricated parties.

Another job completed, she crawled out backwards from the last table. Straightening up, still on hands and knees, she groaned as she placed her hands in the small of her back.

'Can I help you?'

She jerked around so fast at the sound of Lucas's voice she almost fell over.

'You all right?' he asked, lunging forward to catch her before she hit the ground. Shaking him off, she gave him one of her looks. 'I see nothing has changed. Still the same accident-prone Stacey,' he suggested as she staggered to her feet.

'Only when you're around. You jinx me.'

'Can I help?'

'No, thank you. Just put a safe distance between us and I'll be fine.'

'As always,' he observed. 'The status quo must be maintained—Stacey is fine.'

'I *am* fine,' she insisted with an edge of tiredness in her tone.

'Too tired to keep your professional mask on?'

'Something like that,' she admitted with a sigh.

He laughed, and maybe she was overtired, because the sight of that sexy mouth slanting attractively made her want to stop fighting and be friends.

'You've done enough tonight,' he stated firmly as she looked around for something else to do.

'It's my job.'

'Your job is to dance with me,' Luc argued to her astonishment. 'Unless you decide to blatantly ignore a client request, in which case I'll have no alternative other than to report you for being uncooperative.'

'You are joking?'

'Am I? Are you willing to take that risk?'

If this had been ten years ago, she would have challenged him all the way down the line, but she was sure she could see a glint of amusement in his eyes. And why was she fighting anyway? 'You're going to report me because I won't dance with you?' she suggested in a very different tone.

One sweeping ebony brow lifted. 'Sounds fair to me.'

'Everything you say sounds fair to you,' she pointed out, but she was smiling. Luc did that to her. He warmed her when she was in her grumpiest mood, and tonight, looking at him, grumpy was the furthest thing from her mind. 'You are definitely the most annoying man in the world,' she told him.

As well as the most exciting.

'And, thanks for the offer, but I have a lovely placid life and I intend to keep it that way.'

'Boring, do you mean?' Luc suggested, thumbing a chin shaded with stubble as if it were morning and he'd just got out of bed.

'I do not mean boring,' she countered, thoroughly thrown by the way her mind was working. 'I like things just the way they are.'

Luc sucked in his cheeks and the expression in

his eyes turned from lightly mocking to openly disbelieving. 'You don't stay still long enough to know what placid means.' And then he shrugged and half turned, as if he meant to go.

She felt like a hunted doe granted an unexpected reprieve. Badly wanting to prolong the encounter, she was forced to admit that Luc scared her. They'd always had a love-hate relationship: love when they were with the animals they both cared so deeply for, and hate when she saw the easy way Luc wound everyone around his little finger, especially women, forcing teenage Stacey to grit her teeth and burn. How could she not appear gauche compared to the type of sophisticated woman he dated? If she took her clothes off, would she measure up, or would Luc mock her as he used to when she tried to outride him? She couldn't bear it. And…*if* they had sex— heaven help her for even thinking that thought—she would surely make a fool of herself. Having made it her business to be clued up where most things were concerned, short of doing it, it wasn't possible to be clued up about sex, especially with a six-foot-six rugby-playing brother standing in the wings to make sure no half-decent man got near her. When she'd left home for college she hadn't found anyone to match up to Lucas, and the few dates she'd been on had put her off sex for life. Who knew that not everyone showered frequently, or had feet as sexy as she had discovered Luc's were when the three of them used to go swimming in the river? And he wouldn't have patience with a novice. Why should he, when the women she'd seen him with were so confident and knowing? Was it likely he'd give lessons? Hardly, she reflected as she followed his gaze around the room.

'Staff shouldn't be working this late,' he said, turning to her. 'That goes for you too. I'm going to send everyone home.'

'Even me?' she challenged lightly.

'No. You're going to stay and dance. Don't move,' he warned as he went to give the order.

Stacey had done her research and knew Lucas owned this hotel together with several more. He gave the word and came back to her. Everyone apart from a lone guitarist left the ballroom. When Luc returned, he explained that the musician had asked if he could stay on, as he had a flight to catch, and there was no point in going to bed.

'He told me that he'd rather unwind by playing the melodies he loved than spending a few hours in his room, and I get that.' Lucas shrugged. 'I told him to stay as long as he likes. He's not disturbing anyone. Certainly not us,' he added with a long, penetrating look.

Us?

Okay. Get over that. Had she forgotten Luc's love of music? He used to stream music for her to work to at the farmhouse. Maybe she'd added a special significance to the lyrics of the tunes he chose, but the music had helped her escape into another world where there were no grimy floors and dirty dishes.

'I'd welcome anything that drowns out the sound of men's voices,' she would say.

And now?

'Do you always get your way?' she asked, biting her lip to curb a smile.

'Invariably,' Luc admitted, straight-faced. And then he laughed. They both laughed, and what they shared in those few unguarded moments was everything she could wish for: warmth, a past that needed no explanation, and acceptance that they'd both changed, and that life was better now.

'So, why aren't you in bed?' she asked cheekily as the guitarist ended one tune and segued into another.

'I should be,' Luc agreed, but in a way that made her cheeks warm, and suddenly all she could think about was that thwarted kiss all those years ago. Would he push her away if she kissed him now?

'Come on—tell me why you're here.'

'To see you,' he admitted with a wicked look.

'Me?' She laughed, a little nervously now. It always amazed her how the old, uncertain Stacey could return to haunt her at emotionally charged moments like this.

'Why are you so surprised?' Luc asked, bursting her bubble. 'I'm the host of a party you planned. Don't you usually have a debriefing session?'

'Not over a dance,' she said.

He shrugged. 'Why not?'

'We've never danced together before.'

'Let's start a new tradition.'

His eyes were dark and smouldering, while she

was most certainly not looking her best after the busiest of evenings. Was he mocking her? It wouldn't be the first time. They'd mocked each other constantly when she was younger. 'Me dance with you?' she queried suspiciously.

Luc's black stare swept the ballroom. 'Do you see anyone else asking?'

'This had better not be a pity dance,' she warned.

'A pity dance?' he queried.

'Yes, you know, when Niahl used to dance with me whenever I attended those balls you two used to rip up together?'

'The cattle markets?' Lucas frowned as he thumbed his stubble.

'That's what you called them back then,' Stacey agreed.

'What would you call groups of hopefuls with one end in sight?'

'Sheep to the slaughter'

He laughed. 'Of course you would.'

'I was a poor little wallflower,' she insisted, pulling a tragic face. 'No one ever asked me to dance.'

'I wouldn't call you a wallflower. You were more of a thistle. No one wanted to dance with you because you scowled all the time. People want happy partners to have fun with.'

'The type of fun it's better to avoid,' she suggested.

Lucas didn't answer but his expression said that was a matter of opinion.

'Anyway, I didn't scowl,' she insisted, 'and if I

had smiled as you suggest, Niahl would have gone ballistic. He never let anyone near me.'

'Quite right,' Lucas agreed, pretending to be stern while the corner of his mouth was twitching. 'Your brother never liked to see you sitting at a loss, so he danced with you. I don't see anything wrong with that.'

Stacey rolled her eyes. 'Every girl's dream is to dance with her brother, while he scans the room looking for someone he really wants to be with.'

'You're not at a loss now,' Lucas said as he drew her to her feet.

'It appears not,' Stacey answered. She was amazed by how calm she could sound while her senses were rioting from Lucas's firm grip alone. And now their faces were very close. She turned away. 'I'm sure there must be something I should be doing instead of dancing.'

'Yes,' Lucas agreed. His wicked black eyes smiled a challenge deep into hers. 'I plan to discuss that as we dance.'

CHAPTER FOUR

SHE WOULD DANCE and keep a sensible distance.

Lucas was so big, was that even possible?

Even his mouth was sexy, and, like a magnet, was drawing her in. And then there was his scent: warm, clean man, laced with citrus and sandalwood. Damn him for making her feel as if anything he had to say or do was fine by her. She should have stayed until she'd checked every table for lost items, made sure the staff had all gone to bed, and then departed for her room, too tired to think about Lucas.

Where she would continue her lonely existence? She'd made lots of friends since leaving home, but they had their own lives, and carving a village out of a city as big and diverse as London wasn't easy. She had achieved her goal in maintaining her independence and progressing her career, but there was a price to pay for everything, and romance had passed her by. It would have been safer not to dance with Lucas, but he was an anchor who reminded her of good things in her past. Teasing and tormenting him, laughing with him, caring for the animals they loved side by side, had bred an intimacy between them went beyond sex. There was a time when she'd rather have had Lucas tell her that he admired her horsemanship than her breasts, and that was still partly true today. In her fantasies, being held safe in his arms was always the best option, but this wasn't safe. His hands on her body as they danced and his breath on her cheek couldn't remotely be called safe. It was a particular type of torture that made her want more.

Thankfully, she was stronger than that. 'So we've danced,' she declared as if her body wasn't shouting hallelujah, while her sensible mind begged her to leave. 'It's time for me to go to bed.'

'No,' he argued flatly. 'You can't leave now. It would be rude to the musician. He might think we don't like his music.'

She glanced at the guitarist, who was absorbed in his own world. 'Do you think he'd notice?'

Luc's lips pressed down as he followed her gaze. 'I'm sure he would. Do you want to risk it?'

'No,' Stacey admitted. The man had played non-stop during the banquet. Who could deny him his downtime?

'Good,' Lucas murmured, bringing her close.

He'd turned her insides to molten honey with nothing more than an intimate tone in his voice, and the lightest touch of his hands. The sultry Spanish music clawed at her soul, forcing her to relax, and, as so often happened when she relaxed, she thought about the mother she'd lost before even knowing her, and those long, lonely nights of uncertainty when she was a child, asking herself what her mother would have advised Stacey to do to please everyone the following day. She'd failed so miserably on that front, and had begun to wonder if she would ever get it right.

'You're crying.' Drawing his head back, Lucas stared at her with surprise. 'Have I upset you?'

'No. Of course you haven't.' Blinking hard, she shook her head and pasted on a smile.

He captured a tear from her cheek and stared at it as if he'd never seen one before. 'Perhaps you hate dancing with me,' he suggested in what was an obvious attempt to lighten the mood.

'I don't hate it at all,' she said quickly, wishing her mouth would stop trembling. This wasn't like her. She always had her deepest feelings well under control.

'Then what is the matter, Stacey?'

When Lucas talked to her with compassion in his tone he made things worse. She badly wanted to sob out loud now, give vent to all those tears she'd held back as a child. 'I really need to go to bed,' she said, sounding tetchy, which was infinitely better than sounding pathetic. 'I'm tired.'

'You really need to dance,' Lucas argued, tightening his grip around her waist. 'You know what they say about all work and no play?'

'Success?' she suggested with bite.

He refused to be drawn into an argument and

huffed a laugh. 'Even I take time out from work, and so should you.'

Perhaps he was right, she conceded. Being in his arms was so different from what she'd expected that the urge to make the moment last was stronger than ever. She'd been waiting for this all her adult life, and even if the guitarist was doing his best to make her cry, perhaps she needed that too. But not tonight. Tonight was a time for celebration, not tears.

'I'm sorry,' she said. 'It's just that this tune makes me sad.'

'It's good to let your feelings out,' Lucas observed, 'and I'm glad you feel you can do that with me.'

'I do,' she murmured.

He must have given the guitarist a subtle directive, as the mood of the music had changed from unbearably affecting to a passionate, earthy rhythm. They fell into step and began to dance in a way that was far more intimate than before, and as the music climbed to a crescendo it seemed only one outcome was possible. Enjoying Lucas was dangerous because it was addictive. It made her want him in a way that was wholly inappropriate for someone hoping to make an impression on a client.

'I should go.' She pulled away while she still had the strength to do so.

'You should stay,' Lucas argued, and as the guitarist continued to weave his spell, Lucas brought her close enough for their two bodies to become one. She nestled her face against his chest as if she belonged there, as if there had never been any conflict between them, no gulf at all, as if this was how it should be, as if it was right and good.

Dancing with Stacey was harder than he'd thought. Not because she couldn't dance, but because she could; because she was intuitive and could second-guess his every move. Stacey was no longer a vulnerable tomboy on the brink of entering an adult world, but a woman who knew her own mind. She'd looked exhausted when she'd finished work, but there was no sign of tiredness now. If anything, she seemed energised as she moved to the music like a gypsy queen. Though she'd looked close to tears when the music had affected her, determination had since returned to her eyes. And fire. She wanted him, and she wasn't afraid to let him know it.

The ache in his groin was unsustainable. He was seeing her as she was, not as she had been. The urge to feel her naked body under his, to drown in her wildflower scent, and to fist her thick, silky hair as he buried his face in her neck, her breasts—

'Why don't you do it?' she challenged softly.

'Why don't I do what?'

'Kiss me?' she stated bluntly.

She was hyped up on success and impending exhaustion, which meant treating what she said with restraint. In the morning she'd be his friend's little sister again, and would wake up with regrets. 'I've got more sense—'

He hadn't expected such a violent reaction. Springing from his arms, she speared him with a glance, then stalked away. Halfway across the ball-room her stride faltered. Turning to face him, she surprised him even more with an expression that was pure invitation.

Lucas was following and she knew that look on his face. It was the same look as when he chased down a ball in polo, or when a shot of him appeared in the broadsheets after he'd closed some mammoth deal. He was a man on a mission and she was that mis-sion. But they'd meet on her terms and on a ground of her choosing. She'd waited so long for this that her mind was made up. If they only had one night together, she was going to make it the best night of her life. Her body was on fire. He'd done that. Her senses had never been keener. Where Lucas was con-cerned, she'd been honing them for years. Each erog-enous zone she possessed had been teased into the highest state of awareness.

Walking into the now-deserted office that she and the team had been using during the banquet, she left the door ajar. Luc walked in behind her and closed the door securely, before leaning back with a brood-ing expression on his dangerously shadowed face. 'It's been a long time,' he observed in a drawl as lazy as treacle dripping off a spoon. 'And now this?'

She started to say something but thought better of it. No explanations. No excuses. No regrets. The tension in the room was rising. Their gazes were locked. There could be no turning back. The room was so quiet she could hear them breathing. It was as if, having waited all this time, they were balanced on the edge of an abyss, and when they plummeted over that edge they'd both be changed for ever.

'It has been a long time,' she agreed, starting to walk towards him. 'Far too long, Lucas.'

There was an answering spark in Luc's eyes. She was no longer a teenager, or a red-faced intern crushed with embarrassment because she'd ruined his date's dress, or a tomboy arguing the toss with her brother's friend; she was a woman and he was a man. On that level, at least, there was no divide between them.

'Are you sure you know what you're doing?' he said as she stood on tiptoe to cup his face.

'In some ways yes, and in others no,' she admitted truthfully. 'Some might say I'm seducing you.'

'Some?' he queried. 'I'm only interested in what you have to say.'

Black eyes plumbed her soul. 'I want you,' she admitted, as if her whole life had been leading up to this moment. 'For one night.'

'One whole night,' he said, staring down with a glint of humour colouring his black stare. 'Half an hour ago you were determined to go to bed.'

'I still want to go to bed,' she whispered.

Luc hummed as he glanced around the office. 'But not here, surely?'

'Why not?' All the old doubts came crowding in. Was that a genuine comment, or was Lucas looking for a way out?

'Because I don't see a bed,' he suggested dryly.

He made her decision easy when he brushed her lips with his. 'A nightcap?' she suggested. 'Somewhere a little more comfortable than this?'

He didn't answer right away. Stacey's intention was clear. If he accepted there could only be one outcome. He'd resisted temptation where Stacey was concerned for so long he craved sex like a man craving water in a desert. But there was the added complication of his upcoming mountain event. Working side by side would bring them closer still and Stacey could never be some casual fling.

His hunger combined with Stacey's intention to move things forward fast, and in a very different direction, triumphed over any hesitation he might have had. There was nothing safe about entering into the type of situation she was proposing, since he was a man who would happily entertain risk on the polo field, and sometimes even in business, but who would never risk his heart.

Without another word they headed for his penthouse with Stacey in the lead. If she'd been holding his hand, she'd be dragging him. Linking their fingers, he ushered her into his private elevator, which, conveniently, they found waiting on the ballroom level. The instant the doors slid open he backed her inside. Boxing her into a corner, he linked fingers with her other hand. Raising both hands above her head, he pinned her with the weight of his body so he could tease her lips and torment them both as the small steel cocoon rocketed skywards.

Her hands felt wonderfully responsive in his as she made sounds in her throat like a kitten. There was nothing juvenile about her body. That was all woman.

Teasing her lips until she parted them, he kissed her with the pent-up hunger of years. He'd seen this woman grow and endure, survive, and eventually thrive, so this kiss was more than a kiss, it was a rite of passage for both of them.

She whimpered as he mapped her cheeks, her neck, her shoulders, and finally her breasts with his hands, and when he tormented her erect nipples with his thumbnails, she cried out, 'Yes… Oh, yes, please…'

'Soon,' he promised as the elevator sighed to a halt.

He swung her into his arms the moment the doors slid open. It felt so good. She felt so good. Warm and scented with the wildflower perfume he would always associate with Stacey, she was so much smaller than he was, and yet strong in every way. She was perfect, and he had never felt more exhilarated than when he dropped kisses on her face and neck for the sheer pleasure of feeling her tremble in his arms, and hearing her moan with impatience to be one with him.

He pressed his thumb against the recognition pad at the entrance to the penthouse suite and the door swung open.

'Crazy,' she exclaimed as he carried her into the

steel, glass and pale wood hallway. 'How the other half lives,' she added, glancing around.

There was barely a chance to lower her to her feet in his bedroom before the storm. He couldn't wait a moment longer and yanked her close as she reached for him. It was like two titans clashing, both equally fierce. The urgent need for physical satisfaction clawed at their senses, demanding they do something about it fast. Stacey growled with impatience as he unzipped her dress and let it drop to the floor in a pool of silk.

They both tugged at her thong.

'Let me,' she insisted.

He answered the argument by ripping the flimsy lace and casting the remains aside. As he carried her to the bed she was still kicking off her shoes. Papers and files littered the cover so he swept it clear, before laying her down. Discarded jeans, files, a laptop, and a briefcase tumbled to the floor, but he cared for nothing beyond the fact that Stacey's eyes were black, and her lips were swollen from his kisses.

'I want you,' she gasped as he shrugged off his jacket. 'Be quick,' she insisted.

Hooking a thumb into the back collar of his shirt, he tugged it over his head. Her sweeping glance took in his torso and he could only suppose it passed her test as she moistened her lips and reached for him. 'Don't make me wait,' she warned.

Stacey didn't wait. Even he couldn't have freed his belt buckle that fast.

* * *

Whipping Luc's belt out of its loops, she exclaimed with triumph. With another growl, she freed the top button of his trousers and attended to his zipper. That didn't take much persuasion. It flew down as he exploded out of it. Curbing the exclamation of shock that sprang to her lips, she recognised what she'd been missing.

Having never seen anything on this scale before, she took a moment to recalibrate her thinking. Her previous experience was confined to fumbling in the back of a car, or unsuccessful student couplings where both parties were clueless, so this was very different—but then Luc was very different. He was the only man she'd ever really wanted, and here they were.

Wild with need, she drew her knees up and before he had a chance to react she had wrapped them around his waist.

'*Yes! Please! Now!*' she commanded fiercely, her fingers biting into his shoulders.

'But gently,' Luc insisted.

'No!' she fired back, fighting against him trying to dial down the rush. The reality of being hugely inexperienced compared to Luc wasn't relevant. All that mattered was that he wanted her, *really* wanted her, and if that only lasted for a few moments, a minute or an hour, she'd take it.

'Yes. Gently,' he said on a steady breath that she was sure was intended to soothe her. 'I don't want to hurt you. I'm...big.'

A cry flew from her throat. *Big?* Luc wasn't big, he was enormous, but as he dipped and stroked, and then retreated, her confidence grew. 'I'm okay… o*kay*!' she gasped when he pulled back to check she was all right, but it was too late; Luc already had his suspicions.

'Are you a virgin?' He frowned.

'Why?' Her fingers tightened on his shoulders. There were so many emotions colliding inside her, she didn't know what she was, only that Luc was holding her close and she wanted the moment to last a little longer. 'Why do you ask?'

His look was enough. They knew each other too well for her to lie to him. 'I'm not a virgin. Technically,' she added, red-faced.

Luc's eyes narrowed in suspicion. 'Technically? What does that mean?'

'I'm not intact down there,' she blurted.

'Are you sure you want to go ahead with this?'

'Are *you* sure?' she countered, and, with desperation driving her, she tilted forward to make the outcome inevitable. 'You see,' she said in a tone to make light of things, while her mind was spinning as her body battled to accept a new and very different feeling of being occupied, 'I'm in charge.'

'I don't think so, princess.'

A cry of sheer surprise escaped her as Luc cupped her buttocks in his big hands, lifting her into an even more receptive position. Was she ready for this? Could she take him? Could she take all of him?

Encouraging her with husky words in his own

language, Luc rotated his hips to tease her with the promise if not the pressure where she needed it most. Alarm manifested itself in a cry as he sank a little deeper, but then he pulled back. Luc knew exactly what he was doing, and gradually she began to relax. Teasing made her pleasure grow until it became indescribably extreme. Her doubts and fears had disappeared by this time, and all she felt was hunger for more, and then his hands worked some magic, and another type of alarm struck her. 'I can't—'

'You don't have to, princess…'

The word 'wait' was lost in her screams of shocked delight. Release came so suddenly she wasn't ready for it. If it hadn't been for Luc keeping her still to make sure she enjoyed every single beat of pleasure, the cataclysmic waves racking her body might have been less intense. As it was, all she could do was allow them to consume her.

'You've waited a long time for that,' he remarked, dropping kisses on her mouth as her outburst slowly quietened to rhythmical moans of satisfaction.

'Perhaps I have,' she agreed groggily, 'but I won't admit as much to you.'

'And now you want more?' he guessed.

'I'll admit that much,' she agreed. 'But what about you?'

'I can wait.' He frowned. 'And shouldn't you be safely asleep by now?'

'I warned you not to tease.' Summoning up what little strength remained, she balled her hand into a fist and pummelled it weakly against his shoulder.

'You're going to delay that sleep and make time for me?' Luc suggested with a wicked grin tugging at one corner of his mouth.

'I suppose that depends on how efficient you are,' she gasped out, as if she could ever pretend that this feeling of being one was an everyday experience.

Throwing his head back, Luc laughed. 'I can be efficient. Shall I prove it?'

'What do you think?'

'Right now? I prefer actions to thinking.'

She felt warmth flood her veins, knowing they could lie together in perfect harmony, talking and trusting, and—

She must not get too heavily involved. Past experience of trying to give love where it wasn't wanted had not gone well.

'Relax,' he murmured, staring into her eyes to gauge her pleasure in a way that made her feel as if she was the most important thing in the world to him in those moments. It was as if she were standing on the top of a mountain, and no one but him could push her off.

Drawing back, Luc stared down, as though he had to be sure, and then, seeming to have made his decision, he firmed his jaw in a way that made her shudder with desire. He took her slowly and deeply to the hilt. He was so big it was shocking, but wonderful too, and all he had to do was rotate his hips for her to lose control again.

Her pleasure was short-lived, because this time when her screams had quietened Luc said the one thing that could bring her round as fast as if he'd dashed a bucket of ice-cold water in her face. 'I only wish I could make more time for you,' he observed with a concerned look.

The bottomless pit that opened up in front of her this time had nothing to do with the promise of pleasure. It held only the prospect of being alone again. Of course her rational mind accepted that Lucas led a very busy life, but what had been rational between them up to now? Somehow in the throes of passion she'd forgotten he had a job to do and so did she, and that their paths through life were very different.

Sensing the drop in her mood, he did everything he could to reassure her. Kissing her, he soothed her with long, caring strokes. 'I'll see you later...'

'Perhaps you will,' she agreed as he withdrew carefully.

Regret was a double-edged sword. Whatever Stacey felt now or in the future, this was her first time, so he couldn't begrudge a defensive comment. He'd taken the experience with a pleasure so deep and strong, it would fight bitterly, possibly for the rest of his life, with the knowledge that he had nothing to offer her long-term.

Stacey doubted Lucas would make a point of seeing her later. His last glance in her direction might have been one of conflicted regret, or maybe he'd just given her her marching orders. Which hurt like hell when she had given him the only part of her she had never wanted to give to another living soul. But the facts could not be disputed. 'I'll see you later' was the type of thing people said to each other when they didn't want to firm up a date, let alone set a time for another meeting. She'd see him again in the mountains, where it would be all business.

Maybe if she'd been a different person she would have come straight out with it and asked him, *Do you want to see me again?* But the old doubts were never far away.

What made her think Luc wanted anything more than a pleasurable tussle in bed to relax and prepare him for sleep after the banquet? Did she flatter herself that she could hold anyone's interest for longer than it took to give them what they wanted?

Everything had changed, and nothing, she reflected as images of her father and stepmother mocking her attempts to please them slipped unbidden into her mind.

CHAPTER FIVE

Stepping into the empty elevator on the penthouse level before dawn on the night after the banquet, which she had spent with Luca, was an eerie experience. She'd left him glued to his monitor as he responded to emails from across the world. He had an early-morning meeting, he'd told her, so she should get on.

'Oh, okay, then,' she'd said, realising she'd expected something more—a peck on the cheek... Something... Anything.

Pulling herself together, she'd headed out.

It was a special time in the hotel before the morning rush began. The building seemed empty, but that was an illusion as deceptive as Stacey's belief that Luc must feel something after they'd spent the night together. She had no regrets. It had seemed fated somehow. There was no one in the world she would rather have shared that experience with, but Luc had barely looked up when she'd left.

As the elevator dropped like a stone, thinking about how much she believed she'd shared with him, made her throat tighten. Gritting her jaw, she resolved to pull herself together. She had to get over it, and get over him. When she arrived in the mountains she wanted everything to run smoothly, which meant showing no sign of personal distress. She was his party organiser and Luc was the host. And that was all they were to each other.

Thinking back over the night it was fair to say Luc had given no indication that he wanted to see her again, and neither had she. She'd taken a shower. He'd taken a shower. Separately. He'd dressed. She'd prepared for the walk of shame, donning her evening gown, and shunning Luc's offer of a robe before heading back to her room to change. The choice between towelling and silk was easy when she no longer cared.

Tears came when she least expected them. Her emotions were all over the place, Stacey accepted as she braced her balled fists against cold, unyielding steel and willed the doors to open so she could step out into a new day and make a better job of it. Squeezing her eyes tightly shut, she tried to understand why, after getting everything she'd ever wanted with Luc last night—everything she had *thought* she wanted—it still wasn't nearly enough.

His penthouse had never felt empty before, but lacking Stacey's vibrant presence it was just another hotel room. Having showered, he slipped into sweats, and began pacing the sleek, Scandi-style sitting room overlooking Barcelona. The astonishing sights were lost on him. Even the sun shooting its rays above a distant horizon meant nothing to him. He'd never felt like this after making love to a woman. Truthfully, he'd never felt anything. Animal instinct was a powerful driver, and knowing that, he should have slowed things down with Stacey, but his first sight of her after a space of five years had tilted his world on its axis.

What the hell was happening to him?

Staring into the mirror, he raked his hair and growled as he shook his head like an angry wolf. Stubble blackened his face. His hard, unyielding face. Beneath her professional shell, Stacey was still as soft and vulnerable as ever, and damaged by the past. He, of all people, should understand that. But he'd never felt like this before. It was as if everything that had been missing from his life had come pouring in, but too fast, so that instead of tender, protective thoughts, wild, animal passion consumed him.

Planting his fists against cold granite on the breakfast bar, he dipped his head and tightened his jaw. He'd seen too much of Stacey's early life not to care. She'd used him for satisfaction, but he'd hardly been a passive bystander and had never known pleasure like it. Stacey had well and truly turned the tables, and when they met again...*if* they met again...

When they met again, he determined fiercely. For her sake, he'd be cool and distant so as not to mislead her. But was that the best he could do to save her from another cold, unfeeling man? Her father had done enough damage, and he could not bear to do more.

Did she feel anything for him?

Damage from the past cut deep in both of them. Doubt and mistrust were never far away. Lifting his head, he smiled in acknowledgement of this.

But they could change. He could change.

Could he?

The real question was, did he want to?

She was looking forward to the big event in the mountains, and it had to stay that way. How Luc would feel when he saw her again, remained to be seen. Her feelings were unchanged. From day one she had felt something for him—a lot, she admitted—so if he ignored her or, worse, if he was unemotional, and confined their dealings solely to business, it would mean putting on the act of her life.

And she would, she determined as she said goodbye to the team. 'See you in the mountains!' she exclaimed brightly as she wondered why life had to be so complicated.

Because life was tough for everyone, she concluded when she was alone in the room, gathering up her things. Nothing was straightforward for anyone, and, short of locking herself away and never doing anything, there *would* be hurt and disappointment, and pain, but there would be moments of happiness too, so she'd cling to those and get through it. Dreaming of a life with Luc was not only unrealistic, it would be like walking into pain with her eyes wide open. Any thoughts of a long-term relationship between them was a fantasy too far. Luc was a high-flyer while she had barely tested her wings. As far as business was concerned, she was confident he couldn't have any complaints, but when it came to personal feelings... Maybe she'd never know what he felt. Luc had always kept personal matters close to his chest. Niahl's theory was that Luc would never open up, because that would mean confronting the grief of losing his parents. The stresses of business and people who depended on him for their livelihoods, together with concern for his siblings, had robbed him of the chance to grieve.

Niahl was probably right, and Luc had spent so many years regarding her as nothing more than Niahl's annoying little sister that he probably couldn't conceive of her being anything more.

Except for last night.

Which was already behind her.

What happened to your confidence?

She'd left it in his penthouse suite. Luc had restored her confidence in being someone worth spending time with, but one night of passion did not a romance make. Better one fabulous night, she concluded, gritting her jaw. It was more than some people had. Instead of dwelling on what she couldn't make happen, she should concentrate on what she could, which, with the aid of her team, was to create the most fabulous party of the year.

After a tense breakfast meeting during which he could hardly concentrate long enough to sign a multimillion-dollar contract to upgrade the tech for the government of a small country, his thoughts turned back with relief to Stacey. Anything that had happened between them was his fault. He could have resisted and had chosen not to.

Calling the elevator, he stepped into the cab and, leaning back against the wall, closed his eyes. This was the same Stacey who used to wear her hair in braids and give him a hard time at the farm. He smiled as he pictured her at the banquet last night, so determined to make everyone's night a success, including his. A little tired and frazzled around the edges, but definitely all grown up, as she'd proved later in his bed. As far as business went, early reports from his team said the banquet was the best yet.

As he stepped out into the lobby of the glass and steel monument to his success, she consumed his thoughts. His hunger to chart every change in Stacey from gauche ingénue to the professional woman she was today was eating him alive. And he'd never know, because he wouldn't risk getting closer to her. He'd seen enough of her home life to know the journey she'd taken to this point. With no intention of adding to her woes, he'd put distance between them.

His Lamborghini was waiting at the kerb. Tipping the valet, he folded his athletic frame into the car and eased into the morning traffic. His thoughts turned to the day Niahl had left home. Stacey had been too young to follow her brother, and had made such a lonely figure standing at the farm gate waving them off. She'd looked broken. He'd watched in the wing mirror until they'd turned a corner and he hadn't been able to see her any more. It had been a desperate end to an unhappy visit, during which he'd seen her run ragged as she'd tried to care for everyone. It had seemed to him that no one cared for Stacey but her brother, Niahl.

As soon as she'd been old enough, she'd changed her life. A scholarship to a college specialising in the hospitality industry in London had resulted in her graduating as the top student in her year. How could he risk destroying the confidence that had given her by embarking on some ultimately doomed affair? Stacey deserved more than a man who walked away if emotion ever threatened to cloud his rational mind.

Almost four hectic weeks had passed since the memorable encounter with Luc in Barcelona. Planning any party could be a logistical nightmare, but when the venue was in a challenging location Stacey and her team had to work flat out to make sure that everything was delivered well in advance. She'd barely had a moment to breathe, let alone consider what memories Luc had been left with after their passionate night.

After the clamour of the city the serene peace of the mountains was nothing short of a dream come true. The air was cool and clean. Crisp white snow crunched underfoot, and the sky was a flawless, cerulean blue. The small village with its backdrop of towering mountains was like the best picture postcard in the world. The slopes were teeming with skiers, all of whom moved to their own sure, rhythmical pattern, while beginners on the nursery slopes made shakier and more uncertain figures. One thing, however, was common to all. Everyone was smiling.

'What a fabulous atmosphere! What a place to hold a party!' she exclaimed to her companions in the team. 'We're going to have the best time ever here. It's going to be the party of the year.'

Only the final tweaks remained and Stacey was as certain as she could be that Lucas would love what they had planned. *Lucas.* She was desperate to see him, and dreading it too. What if he—?

No. Don't think that way. Only positive thoughts from now on.

They had to meet, and she'd take it from there. It wouldn't be easy with the brand of his lips on her mouth and the memory of his hands on her body, but what was easy? Nothing worth having, that was for sure.

'We'll make this event something the Da Silva guests never forget, and for all the right reasons,' she told the team. 'How beautiful is this?' she exclaimed, turning full circle. 'Let's get settled in, and then we can make a start.'

The success of any team depended on its leadership. That was something Lady Sarah had drummed into her right at the start, so, whatever Stacey's personal feelings about Lucas, she had to get on with things for the sake of the team.

'There will be a few more hurdles to cross here than we had in the city,' Stacey observed later when she and the team were seated around a boardroom table in an office the hotel had made available for them. 'The weather, for one thing,' she said, glancing out of the window. The quaint, pitched-roofed buildings had been covered in deep mantles of snow when they'd arrived, but now they were gradually fading out of sight. A drift of snowflakes falling like a veil was growing heavier by the minute, while the flawless blue sky that had so impressed her was rapidly turning to unrelieved grey. 'I should get out and scout the various locations while I still can,' she said, drawing the meeting to a close. 'Take the night off. I'm going to need everyone firing on all cylinders tomorrow.'

'What about you?' a colleague piped up.

'I'll rest when I'm reassured about our venues. Until then…?' She shrugged.

'Keep in touch.'

'I will,' she promised.

The village proved to be a fascinating place with its glitter and sparkle, but what struck Stacey more was the resilience of visitors and residents alike as they crowded the pavements in what were undeniably extreme weather conditions.

Still, everyone was dressed for it, Stacey reasoned, admiring the beautifully decorated shop windows as she strode past in her snow boots and Party Planners padded jacket. She was heading for the gondola station as, not only was there to be a party down here, but a reception higher up the mountain at Luc's ski lodge, as well as a firework display and a torchlit procession down the mountain. Pausing briefly to adjust her snow goggles, she studied the statue of a miniature couple in one of the windows. Placed outside the model of a typical chalet, both figures were wearing skis and staring up at each other in apparent rapture.

I should have learned to ski, she mused silently. Too late now. But the gondola would take her where she needed to be. She could just step in and out, no problem.

Craning her neck when she reached the station, she tried to spot Luc's eyrie. It was supposed to be the biggest chalet on the mountain. She thought of it as his castle, his fortress, his ivory tower. But she couldn't see anything as low cloud and the misting of snow had blotted out the upper reaches of the route the gondola would take.

What if the gondola stopped running? How would they transport the guests?

There was time, Stacey reasoned. They had a good few days before the party. Surely the weather would have improved by then?

The hotel manager had told her that Lucas had arrived by helicopter that same morning. Her heart went crazy all over again, just as it had the first time she'd heard it. 'Nothing deters him,' the hotel manager had said. 'Bad weather has been forecast, but Señor Da Silva is an expert pilot, so he knows all about timing to escape the worst of any oncoming storm.'

Yes, he would, she'd thought then. Niahl had warned her that the weather could be unpredictable but that this resort had some of the most challenging slopes in the world, which was what had attracted Lucas to the village in the first place. It would, she mused.

Would Luc be thinking about her, as she was thinking about him?

Only in as much as he might wonder if she and the team had arrived before the weather closed in, she concluded. She hadn't heard from him since Barcelona, confirming her belief that their night together meant more to her than it did to him. Of course he'd take for granted the fact that she'd get on with things. And why shouldn't he? She wanted him to know he could rely on her, and that Party Planners would give him the event of the year.

She paused at the foot of the steps leading up to the gondola station. Her pulse jagged at the thought of seeing Luc again. Dragging deep on the ice-cold air, she hunched her shoulders into her jacket and drove forward into the wind. Behind her, vehicles with snow chains were crawling along. Even they were having difficulty negotiating the road. But what she'd started, she would finish. All she needed was a quick look-see so she could brief the team, and then she'd head straight back down the mountain to take a hot bath and have a good sleep before the real work began tomorrow.

CHAPTER SIX

STACEY ONLY REALISED what she'd taken on as the packed gondola transporting skiers to their chalets on the higher levels left its berth on the lower station. It was one thing agreeing to what had seemed a perfectly reasonable request by the Da Silva team, to hold a party in the main village before transporting guests up the mountain for the grand finale of fireworks and a torchlit descent. There was no doubt that the infrastructure was here to support that. But when the weather closed in as it had done today, she could only be grateful that she'd taken the precaution of having everything delivered in good time for the party. She doubted anything else would get through.

Luc had intimated through the head of his team that he had a novel idea for ferrying guests up the mountain for the champagne reception. Stacey had yet to learn what that was, and had put in an urgent request for more information so she could plan for whatever needed to be done.

Firming her jaw, she stared out of the window. There were always challenges, but this took things to the wire. As the ground dropped away the wind picked up and whistled around the swaying car. None of her companions seemed concerned, so she made herself relax and wait until that blissful moment when she was back on solid ground.

Snow was falling steadily when she joined the crowds streaming out of the station. She had a map but it wasn't much use now the street had disappeared beneath a thick white carpet. Seeing a ticket booth, she stopped to ask directions and was told that she couldn't miss the Da Silva chalet as it was the largest private structure in town. 'Will the gondola continue to run?' she asked, staring up at the leaden sky.

'Of course,' she was told. 'Only a white-out or heavy winds could stop the service, and this weather system is supposed to move on.' A glance at the sky seemed to confirm this. A big patch of blue had broken through the cloud. Thanking the clerk, she took the precaution of donning a pair of high-performance ski goggles to prevent snow-blindness and set off, but she had barely made it out of the station before a strong wind kicked up. The patch of blue she'd been so relieved to see soon disappeared behind a fresh bank of cloud and these clouds were thicker and darker than before.

Weather in the mountains was known to be unpredictable. Could anyone accurately predict the capricious path of Mother Nature? Somehow, she doubted it.

A heavy silence gathered around her as she

trudged along. Everyone else seemed to have re-treated into their houses or hotels, and even those buildings had turned ghostly in the half-light. Her heart was racing. The snow was falling so heavily now, it was like a thick white curtain in front of her face. Her heart was racing. She'd heard enough horror stories to know she should be concerned. She couldn't even be sure if she was walking in a straight line or going around in circles. Luc's chalet was supposed to be close to the station, and, though it might be the largest private home in the area, if she couldn't see the other buildings, what hope did she have of finding it?

Adjusting her neck warmer so it covered her mouth and nose, she bent her head into the wind and slogged on. Going back wasn't an option. When she stopped and turned to try and get her bearings, the gondola station had disappeared. Tugging off a thick ski glove with her teeth, she located her phone and tried to call her colleagues in the village. No signal. There was only one option left, and that was to keep on walking in the hope that something would come into view, though that didn't seem likely in this all-encompassing sea of white.

'Hello! *Hello!*' she called out, panic-stricken. 'Can anyone hear me?'

Silence answered her call.

'Hello! *Hello!*' she repeated at the top of her lungs. 'Is anyone out here?'

She stood motionless in the snow with her arms crossed over her chest as she tried to slap some life into her frozen limbs. There was not a sound to be heard other than the wailing of the wind and the deceptively silky whisper of deadly snowflakes.

And then…

Was she dreaming?

'Hello!' she cried out wildly, feeling certain she'd heard a faint sound in the distance. 'Hello?' she called again.

She tried to locate the source of the sound, but it seemed to come from everywhere and nowhere at once. 'I'm over here!' she bellowed tensely.

'Stay where you are! Don't move. I'm coming to get you.'

'Luc?' Relief engulfed her.

'I said, stay where you are.'

His voice was harsh, imperative, quashing her relief, and turning it to exasperation that of course it had to be Luc who found her.

'Stacey? You have to keep shouting so I can find you.'

The wind tossed his voice around so it was impossible to tell which direction he was calling from. 'Hello! Hello!' she called out in desperation. 'I'm over here.'

'Don't move. I can hear you. Keep shouting…'

But his voice sounded fainter as he was walking away from her. 'I'm over *here*,' she yelled, frantic with fear that he might walk straight past her. 'Please…' Her voice broke with sheer terror that, having been found, she might be abandoned again. And then, quite suddenly, they were standing face to face. Regardless of anything that had gone before, she catapulted herself into his arms. 'Thank God you found me!'

'*Dios!* Thank God I did. What on earth are you doing up here?'

'Researching.'

'Couldn't that have waited until tomorrow?'

'I like to be prepared.'

'But you've only just arrived,' Luc pointed out. 'My people gave me your schedule,' he explained.

'The team is resting,' she confirmed, 'but I want to be informed, ready to brief them in the morning.'

Luc frowned down at her. 'There's dedication to duty, and then there's obsession,' he observed. 'Didn't it occur to you that you should be resting too?'

'Pot, kettle, black?' she suggested. 'Do you hang around when an important deal is on the table? No. I didn't think so. And I wouldn't be here at all if I hadn't checked first that the gondolas would be running in spite of the weather.'

'In fairness, no one could have predicted this,' Luc agreed, driving forward. 'The gondola station has only just closed.'

'Closed?' Stacey exclaimed. 'How do I get down the mountain?'

'You won't—not tonight, at least.'

'A hotel, then,' she said hopefully, looking about.

'All the hotels are full of people who are stranded,' Luc explained.

'So where *are* you taking me?'

'Does it matter?' Grabbing hold of her arm, he urged her along. 'Come on, we'll freeze if we stay here.'

Against her better judgement where Luc was concerned, she felt safe for the first time since coming up the mountain. And optimistic for some reason. She felt way too much of everything, Stacey concluded as she admitted, 'This is not how I expected us to meet.'

'I'm sure not,' Luc agreed, forced to shout as he drove them both on against the battering snow. 'You're lucky I was checking the progress of evacuating skiers, and making sure the slopes were clear, or we wouldn't be here.'

'Where exactly *are* we?' she asked. 'How do you even know where we're going?' Having stared about, she couldn't be sure of anything but an unrelieved vista of white.

'I just know where I am,' Luc said with confidence. 'In-built GPS, I guess.'

She wouldn't put anything past him. 'I'm sorry to have caused you so much trouble.'

'Not your fault,' he said brusquely. 'It's been called the freak storm of the century. No one saw this coming.'

Reassured that he didn't think her completely reckless in venturing up the mountain, she asked another question. 'Do you have a phone signal at your chalet? I need to reassure the team I'm okay.'

'I have a landline,' Luc confirmed, 'though mobile lines are dead. You can ring the hotel and leave a message.'

'Sure?'

'Of course.'

'That's very kind of you.'

This was too polite, she mused as Luc steered her away to the left; a bit like the calm before the storm.

'My chalet's over here.'

'So close,' she exclaimed with surprise.

'As close as the black ski run where I found you.' Luc's voice held irony and humour in matching amounts. 'You might have had a shock if you'd gone that way.'

'Terrifying,' she agreed. 'Particularly as I can't ski.'

'Nor can I without skis,' Luc pointed out dryly.

In all probability, Luc had saved her life. 'I can never thank you enough for finding me.'

'We'll find a way.'

Her heart almost leapt out of her chest. Her brain said it was a throwaway remark, but it was still Luc speaking. She hoped he'd say more. He didn't. Locking an arm around her waist, he steered her until finally he half carried her up a slope that had probably been steps to his chalet before the snows came.

'Thank you,' she said as he steadied her on the ground as the impressive entrance door swung open.

'You'll have plenty of chances to thank me,' he observed with some irony. 'You won't be going anywhere tonight. Neither of us will. You'll have to stay in the chalet with me.'

Left with that alarming thought, she smiled as obliging staff gathered on the doorstep to greet them.

Without exception, they were relieved to see Lucas return safely. He introduced Stacey to his housekeeper, a rosy-cheeked older woman called Maria, who wanted nothing more than to take Stacey under her wing, but they all paused in the same instant as a thin wail cut through their greeting.

'Did you hear that?' Stacey asked.

'Go inside while I take a look around,' Luc instructed.

'No way. I'm coming with you. It isn't safe to be out on your own tonight.'

'Says you?' he countered with a devastating smile. 'Do you think two of us will be safer?'

'Two will stand more chance of finding someone stranded.'

'No.' He shook his head. 'You're freezing. Go inside.'

'I can last a little longer, and if there is someone out there, we have to find them.'

'You have to call your team,' he reminded her.

'And I will, just as soon as I get back.'

Luc frowned. 'That sounds like an animal in distress…'

'Let's go,' Stacey insisted, tugging on his arm.

An hour later, she and Maria were tending a cat after a most astonishing encounter in Luc's boot room. Two calls later, and Stacey had informed her team that she was safe and they should stay where they were. 'I'll give you an update tomorrow,' she promised.

'Bath. Now,' Luc instructed from the doorway. 'I

won't be answerable for your well-being if you don't take my advice.'

'I didn't ask you to be answerable.' She couldn't bring herself to add, *I'm fine. I can look after myself*, as the blizzard had clearly proved her wrong about that.

'Lucky for you, I'm still going to care about your welfare,' Luc said in a tone that made her think he was speaking as her brother's friend, rather than as her lover. 'Just remember—you're in my house and I'm in charge. No arguments,' he added in a mock-stern tone. 'And when you take a shower be sure to run it cold, or you'll burn yourself. Even on the coldest setting the water's going to feel warm to you. It's only safe to increase the temperature when the water starts to feel chilly to you. When you're confident everything's back to normal you can take a bath. Don't rush. I'll be doing the same thing.'

He was almost out of the door when he thought better of it and turned around. 'You did well tonight. That could have been a person, and a cat is no less deserving of our care. Mountain rescue will be on the case by now. They're a lot better equipped than I am for this sort of thing, so you can relax. I'll call them to let them know the area we covered, and then we can safely leave them to it. I'll join in later if they need me.'

'Then so will I,' Stacey insisted.

'No, you won't. You can't ski, and you don't know the mountains. You'll only get in the way. Stay here. You were brave tonight. Don't be foolish now.'

'I wasn't brave, I was scared to death,' she admitted. 'That's why I had to go out again, in case there were others trapped like me.'

'You're very honest,' he observed.

She shrugged. 'I try to be.'

Stacey, Stacey, Stacey! What was she doing to him? Lucas reflected as he paced the great room, attempting not to think of her naked beneath the shower. He'd passed the time while she'd been warming up, making calls to reunite the cat with its owner, and to alert the mountain rescue team to their actions. The search chief had praised Stacey for her bravery. Any visitor who, having found safety, set out again in such terrible conditions to help others was worthy of a commendation, he'd said. 'I'll pass that on to her,' Luc had promised.

No one got through to him like Stacey, who had made a mockery of his intentions to save her from him. Saving her *for* him made more sense right now—especially when, in a moment of complete madness, he had felt moved to enclose her face in his hands in the boot room to give her a brief, reassuring kiss—on the cheek, but still... What the hell had he been thinking? It was bad enough they were here, trapped together in his chalet overnight, without him making things worse. So much for good intentions! She'd ridden roughshod over his control.

What alternative did he have? With many of his guests having arrived early to make the most of their trip, he could use all the people he could get, both up here and down at the hotel. Stacey's team was in place in the village while she was here, ready to act on any changes to her plans for the party brought on by the weather.

At least she appeared to be following orders for once. *For now.* Maria had reported back that warm clothes had been delivered to Stacey's suite of rooms, and she was enjoying a bath. She could stay one night, but no longer. His libido couldn't take it. He had nothing to offer Stacey that she'd be interested in. Money, jewels, fashion meant nothing to her. Her practical nature was fulfilled by her rigorous working regime, but when it came to the personal side of things, she was a dreamer, a romantic, who, now they'd had sex, would expect more than he could give.

A beautiful woman had sought refuge under his roof, but all he could think about was keeping his thoughts and feelings locked up tight.

That wasn't strictly true, was it? However many times he told himself that this was Stacey, the imp who used to plague him at her father's farm, his straining groin begged to differ. Rearranging his over-packed jeans, he grimaced. He couldn't even trust himself to guide Stacey to her bedroom, and had left that task to Maria. Having known her intimately, he wanted her again, and that want was like a fury drilling away inside him to the point where he found it impossible to concentrate on anything else.

He had to have her. It was as simple as that.

Would it be so simple for Stacey?

A humourless laugh escaped him at the thought that she was quite capable of turning him down. Stacey wasn't like anyone else he'd ever known. She lived life by her own rules, and his gut instinct warned him that obeying him would figure nowhere in her plans, a thought that only sharpened his appetite.

He glanced at the thick fur rug in front of the hearth, longing to hear her moan beneath him as her eyes and mouth begged him to take her again. To feel her hips straining to meet his; to have her until she couldn't stand; to bring her more pleasure than she'd ever known—

Stop! Get over this obsession with Stacey and accept that she's here to work!

How was he supposed to forget the telling signs of arousal in her darkening eyes when she looked at him? Or his desire to kiss every inch of her body? The disappointment on her face when he'd passed her over to Maria had told him everything: Stacey wanted him as much as he wanted her.

Get over it. Forget it.

Pouring a stiff drink, he gulped it down. Discarding the glass, he gave a roar of frustration as he planted his fist into the wall.

CHAPTER SEVEN

BACK TO SQUARE one with Lucas?

Possibly, Stacey accepted as Maria showed her to her room. She touched her lips. Having returned with relief to the chalet, Luc had seemed almost eager to hand her over to someone else, while she was still obsessing over the ice crystals outlining his mouth, and the frosting of snow dampening the thick whorls of pitch-black hair escaping his ski hat. Having so recently been familiar with every naked inch of him, she found it strange now to think how awkward she would have felt if she'd reached up to push back his hair. She touched her mouth again, remembering.

As if she could forget.

The heated racks made the boot room a cosy space to strip off outer clothes, but Luc had shown no interest in conversation. Appearing lost in thought, he'd tugged off his gloves and tossed them on a chair. His boots had gone onto the racks, and he'd grunted at her to do the same with hers. Then he'd stilled and turned to look at her.

'Well done, you,' he'd murmured, frowning as if he couldn't quite believe she'd insisted on going with him into the snow.

'And you,' she'd said. 'Thank you…'

Another few long moments had gone by as they had stared into each other's eyes, and then, enclosing her cheeks in his big, strong hands, Luc had kissed her, but not as Luc the lover, more as a caring friend, which had almost been worse than not being kissed at all.

'And this will be your room while you're staying with us, Señorita Winner.'

'Thank you so much. It's beautiful,' she said, jolting back to the present as she realised Maria was waiting for a reaction to a most beautiful suite of rooms.

'Please do remember what Señor Da Silva told you about the shower,' Maria cautioned as she opened the door on a fabulous marble-lined bathroom.

'I won't forget anything Señor Da Silva said,' Stacey promised, which was the absolute truth. Memories were almost certainly all she'd have to take away from here.

Climbing out of a deliciously warm scented bath some time later, she swathed herself in towels, and began to pace her room. Like everything else she'd seen in the chalet so far, the guest suite was the last word in luxury. Everything was operated from a central console by the bed. She would expect nothing less of a tech billionaire. Exactly like his expert kisses—kisses that conveyed so much, whether that be kisses of reassurance, or kisses in the height of passion—Luc was a genius. It was as simple as that.

She'd rather have that genius here at her side, celebrating life, than be raising the bed with the flick of a switch, and lowering it again, just because she could. It wasn't enough to *try* and stop thinking about Lucas when he occupied every corner of her mind. It was all too easy to picture them both on the bed—intimate, close, loving, kissing. Turning her back on the offending mattress, with its lush dressing of crisp linen sheets and cashmere throws, she wished fervently he could open up enough for her to know if this ache in her heart was futile.

Had she given up?

She stared into the mirror. That wasn't the question.

This was the question: Was she wasting her time pining for a man who might never reveal himself to anyone?

There's only one thing for it...

Seduce him?

Honestly, sometimes her reckless inner self came up with some extraordinary ideas.

Why not? that same inner voice demanded. *You've got the tools, now go to work!*

She laughed as she pushed away from the console table beneath the mirror. Seducing Lucas Da Silva would certainly be a first.

Maria was as good as her word and had dropped off a set of sweats for Stacey to wear. Fortunately, they fitted, along with the underwear, which was still in a pack from the store. She took her time going downstairs to join Lucas, as she wanted to have a proper look around. Everything she'd imagined about Lucas Da Silva's mountaintop eyrie was improved upon. She'd seen a lot of fabulous homes with the team, but nothing close to approaching this. Floodlights were on outside, revealing the smooth carpet of snow with its shadowy mountain peaks beyond. The sky had cleared and the moon was shining brightly, adding to the illumination that revealed a heated outdoor swimming pool with steam rising, and a veranda overlooking the ski slopes where the torchlit procession would take place.

'Wow,' she murmured.

'You approve?'

She swung around. 'You spying on me?'

Luc's low growl came from a shady corner of the room. 'I'm having a drink.'

Now she saw him properly, firelight flickering off the harsh planes of his face as he lounged back in a big, comfortable chair.

'Come and join me,' he suggested. 'Unless you've got something better to do?'

She hummed, and then said lightly, 'You're in luck. I can't think of anything better to do right now. Give me enough time, and maybe I will.'

'Come over here. I've got a message for you.'

'For me?' She couldn't resist crossing the room to sit by Lucas anyway. Hadn't she vowed to bring matters between them to some sort of conclusion?

Padding barefoot over luxurious rugs that made the mellow wooden floor seem even homelier, she couldn't help but marvel at the easy mix of tech and comfort he'd achieved in this house. In spite of the emotional turmoil raging inside her, there was a good feeling in the building. It was easy to see why Luc loved his mountain retreat. He could relax here.

'Drink?' he suggested.

'Water, please.' She needed her wits about her.

'As you wish. I'll open champagne, if you prefer?'

'Perhaps after the party, when, hopefully, I'll have something to celebrate.'

'Hopefully?' he probed with a keen look.

'When we'll *both* have something to celebrate,' she amended in answer to his question. 'You mentioned a message to pass on to me?' she prompted.

'Ah, yes. I spoke to mountain rescue and the team was full of praise for you. They wanted you to know, that's all.'

'Thank you.' She couldn't pretend that didn't light a glow inside her. It was always good to be appreciated. 'I hope you told them why I did it, and how scared I was.'

'I didn't need to.' He shrugged. 'Only fools don't feel fear.'

'If you can't experience emotion, what do you have?'

'You're asking the wrong person,' Luc assured her.

There was an ironic twist to his mouth as she went to warm her hands in front of the blazing log fire while he fixed their drinks.

'I love your photographs,' she said in an attempt to break the sudden tension. They showed Luc and his brothers playing polo, and there was another photograph of him and his siblings, though not one single image of his parents. She knew their death had been a tragic accident, but found it strange that he wouldn't want to be reminded of happier days.

'Water?' he prompted.

'Thank you.' A glance into shuttered eyes warned against asking too many personal questions about Luc's photographs, or any that she might perceive as missing.

'I think hot chocolate would be better than water, don't you?'

She knew him well enough to suspect that this was a ploy to change the subject completely, rather than to provide her with an alternative drink.

'That would be good,' she agreed. 'I'd love one. Thank you.'

How prim she sounded, when all she could think about was his hands on her body and his mouth on her lips, and the pleasure they'd shared. She must be a better actress than she'd thought.

Would she ever get used to the sight of him? Stacey wondered as Luc picked up the phone to call Maria. Freshly showered with his thick hair still damp and catching on his stubble, Luc was a magnificent sight. Her heart pounded with bottled-up emotion, while her body was more forthright when it came to aching with lust.

But how did he feel about her? Could anyone read

the thoughts behind those enigmatic black eyes? Somehow, she doubted it.

'Your wish is my command,' Luc assured her in the same soft drawl as Maria tapped lightly on the door.

His faint smile sent shivers coursing down her spine, and the moment Maria had left them she felt compelled to ask, 'Is my every wish really your command?'

'What do you think?' Luc asked.

She shrugged and smiled with pure disbelief.

'But of course it is,' he assured her wickedly.

A few moments later they were seated in front of the fire, each with an aromatic mug of cocoa in their hands. To any onlooker, it was a cosy scene, a safe scene, with two people who knew each other well. Stacey had relaxed, and in doing so had decided to forget her reckless plan to show Lucas how much she wanted him. Why set herself up for failure, when things were going so well? Did she always have to stick her chin out? Couldn't she for once keep quiet and say nothing? Hadn't she vowed on the day she left home that she would never be pushed aside again? Her intention was to be useful and to help people, and wasn't that better? Didn't it give her a warm feeling inside? Why lay her heart on the line now? Her reckless self could take a hike, she concluded. With a career to foster, and a life to live long after tonight was over, she had safer things to do with her time than seduce Lucas.

'What about supplies in the village?' she asked, determined to turn her mind back to business.

'Does everyone have what they need? I've ordered in enough to withstand a siege, so please tell me if I can help.'

'I will,' Luc assured her, 'but I doubt it will be necessary.' Relaxing back, he explained. 'All the mountain villages are self-sufficient. They have to be prepared for weather like this, but I'll let them know of your offer,' he promised.

As Luc sipped hot chocolate thick enough to stand a spoon in, she dwelt on him. It was inevitable. Thoughts about business were vital to her peace of mind, but with each minute that passed he was becoming increasingly vital to her existence.

Warm chocolate was slipping down her throat like a delicious promise of more pleasure to come, and Luc was a big source of pleasure.

'What are you smiling about?' he asked.

'Me? Just relaxing. Okay, the party,' she admitted when he raised a brow. Just not the type of party Luc was imagining.

And from there the fantasies came thick and strong. He'd showered and changed into banged-up jeans with frayed edges brushing his naked feet—how could feet be so sexy? she asked herself—and a soft black cashmere sweater that clung to his powerful shoulders, emphasising his strength and musculature like a second skin, and she wanted to stroke him, smell him, touch him, taste him. The scent of something citrusy he'd used in the shower was clearly discernible above the tang of wood smoke and the sugary smell of chocolate. He'd pushed his sleeves back, revealing deeply tanned forearms like iron girders, shaded with just the right amount of dark hair. He was a magnificent sight and she wanted him. The fact that Lucas had always been completely unaware of his staggering appeal only made him all the more attractive to Stacey.

'I'd better take that mug before you drop it,' he said.

Realising it had tipped at a perilous angle while she was lost in her thoughts, she laughed. 'I'm going to lick out every last drop first.' When she passed it over to him their fingers touched, and Luc's heat seeped into her. Who was seducing whom here? Her nipples responded on cue, as did the rest of her aching body.

'Now we eat,' he said, which snapped her back to reality. 'You need food.'

So much for reality! Being free from consequences, fantasies were more enjoyable. And, yes, she was playing with fire sitting close to Luc when she could be safely asleep in the guest wing, but she preferred playing with fire to kicking around cold embers in the morning.

When she stretched and grimaced, he commented. 'You could use a massage. Cold does that to your muscles.'

'Are you offering?' She gave him a sideways look while her heart started banging in her chest.

'If you like,' Luc said matter-of-factly. 'A good rub down,' he suggested.

'I'm not your horse.'

'Clearly,' he observed.

She laughed. They both laughed, and she had to tell herself that the attractive curve on Luc's mouth was just his way, and, though she was staying here overnight, she was as safe from him as she would be in a convent.

'Penny for them?' he probed, shooting a smouldering look her way.

She drew herself up. 'You can't know all my secrets.'

'Let's start with one.'

'Says the man who never reveals a single detail about his life?'

Luc shrugged. 'I asked first.'

'Okay,' she agreed. 'You asked for it, so here's one. What happened to my horse? What happened to Ludo?'

He sat back.

'Don't pretend you don't know. And don't keep me waiting for your answer, or I'll know it's bad news. That horse meant the world to me. He was the only friend I—' She broke off. 'Well?' she demanded after a few seconds of silence had passed. 'Tell me.' She braced herself.

'Ludo,' Luc murmured.

'Well, at least you remember his name.'

He frowned. 'Of course I remember his name.'

'So?' she pressed.

'Your pony is having a very happy retirement.'

Tension flooded out of her. 'Go on…' She sat forward eagerly.

'He's at stud siring some of the finest foals in the world. You don't need to worry about Ludo. If you asked him, I doubt he'd want to be anywhere but with his harem on my *estancia*.'

'I'll ask him to confirm that the next time I see him,' she teased, and then she thought of something else. 'Do you still ride him?'

'All the time,' Luc confirmed.

'Good. I can imagine the two of you together.' One so fiery, and one so deep. They belonged together; deserved each other for all the right reasons, and she could see now that something that had hurt her at the time had done Luc and her beloved horse the world of good. 'Ludo would be lost without regular exercise.'

'As would I,' Luc assured her, not troubling to hide the wicked glint in his eyes.

'I wouldn't know about that,' she said, and before he had the chance to speak she put her hand up to stop him. 'And I don't want to know. Just so long as Ludo's happy, that's okay with me.'

They fell silent after that, reminding Stacey that, however much she longed for things to be easier between them, Lucas would always be intractably welded to honour and dignity, and, though he would quite happily talk about the horses they both loved, or the parties Stacey arranged for him, their encounter in Barcelona had been a one-off that he almost certainly regretted.

And yet...

When their glances clashed and he didn't look

away, she got the feeling that he would like to kiss her. Whether it was another of her fantasies, she couldn't tell. And if he did kiss her, she guessed it would be a reassuring kiss and not the way he'd kissed her in Barcelona.

'Food,' he reminded her. 'You must be hungry by now?'

'Starving,' she confirmed.

The tension between them released as he asked what she'd like and they talked easily about what to eat. 'When we've finished you can go straight to bed.'

'Yes, sir.' She gave him a mock salute. 'Any more instructions?'

'That covers it,' he said.

And…was she mistaken, or was that a glint of humour in his eyes? Either that or a reflection of the fire. Why couldn't Luc get it through his head that she was a grown woman with feelings and emotions? Just because he was an emotion-free zone… Or was he? Sometimes she suspected that his feelings, long since bottled up inside him, were longing for a trigger to let them out.

CHAPTER EIGHT

Dios! Each time he saw her he wanted to do a lot more than kiss her. When he'd found her in the snow his world had tilted on its axis. The thought of losing her was insupportable.

'Lucas?'

'What?' Her voice held a concerned note that made him feel bad for locking her out. If there was one person who could undo him it was Stacey, and those memories were better where they were, buried deep. Easing back on the sofa, he spread his arms across the back in an attitude of apparent unconcern.

'You looked so tense,' she remarked, frowning. 'You were actually scowling—not that I haven't seen that expression before. Is something wrong?'

Yes, you're *wrong*, he thought. He should be looking to settle down and start a dynasty to perpetuate Da Silva Inc, but when that time came he'd choose a woman bred for the role, someone sparkling and superficial who he couldn't hurt.

'I'm hungry,' he said with a shrug. 'And you know what I'm like when I'm hungry.'

'Bear? Sore head?' she suggested. And then, without warning, she sprang off the sofa. 'Come on, then…' She held out her hand to take his. 'Let's eat. I'll get no sense out of you until we do.'

He stood, but he didn't make any attempt to hold her outstretched hand. Any contact between them was dangerous. He'd learned there was no such thing as an innocent kiss between him and Stacey, and she deserved a lot more than he could offer.

It was a relief to find himself at the breakfast bar where he could occupy himself with the business of eating rather than dwell on the prospect of sex with Stacey. She helped by chatting about details for the upcoming party, but every now and then she'd look at him with eyes full of compassion, and that wasn't very helpful. She was waiting for him to confide in her, tell her things he'd never told anyone, things he hadn't even confronted himself. Neither of them made any reference to their recent kiss, though, while she might have found it easy to put that behind her, he still brooded on it.

Eventually she sighed, as if she'd given up on him. 'Sorry, but I have to get some sleep,' she said, standing up to go. 'You've been amazing. You saved my life.' And before he knew what she was doing, she leaned forward to brush a kiss against his cheek. It was such a little thing, but long-hidden feelings squirmed inside him. No one kissed him like that. No one had for a long time.

'Okay, goodnight,' she said. 'Try and get some sleep.'

'You too,' he encouraged. *Before I yank you close and kiss the breath out of your body.* 'You've had quite an ordeal today.'

'Not as bad as the cat,' she said dryly.

'Ah, the cat,' he murmured, remembering how tender she'd been with the animal. That memory dredged up more. His parents, his siblings. It was definitely time for Stacey to go. Carrying their plates to the counter, he kept his back turned. 'We both need sleep,' he agreed, but more sharply than he had intended. He felt bad for snapping, but memories were dangerous things. His were better left undisturbed.

When her footsteps faded, he stood in the great room surveying what he could see of the village. Snow had stopped falling, though it had left everything cloaked in white. His best guess was that they would be cut off from the village for a few days. A lot could happen in that time. Yes, a party could be held, and guests entertained. Anything beyond that he would put from his mind.

Rest? Rest was unlikely with Stacey in the next room. If the hotels hadn't been full he'd have shipped her out, but they were where they were. He'd be shovelling snow in the morning, too busy to think of anything else, he reassured himself. Then he would liaise with his people to make sure they had everything covered for the party. The last he'd heard there were no more supplies getting through to the village. He could only be glad Stacey was so well organised.

Stacey...

There she was again. Each time he thought it was possible to stop thinking about her, she invaded his mind. He just had to face facts. The woman she had become was not simply more of a challenge than the tomboy she used to be, but a damn sight more attractive too.

Stacey's usual upbeat mood was flagging as she flopped into bed. Why would Lucas never open up? Instinct told her he'd never move on until he did. And though building a monstrous business was huge credit to him, where was his personal life? Did he have one? Didn't he want one? Or wasn't he capable of building something requiring feelings and giving his all, and risking his heart?

You're a fine one to talk.

Yup. That was a fair accusation. But this was about Lucas, not about Stacey.

Even with all the complications, she loved being with him. The rescue spoke volumes about him. He was a very special individual, and their relationship, such as it was, was very special to her. Sex had been extraordinary; far more pleasure, and infinitely more emotional investment than she had expected.

She smiled, remembering the moment they'd found the cat. Cradling the small, half-frozen animal had woken her heart. Maybe she should get a cat. However fabulous this accommodation and however successful her life, it didn't make up for the stark fact that she was alone.

So change things.

Change things? Her mouth tilted at a disbelieving angle as her inner voice had its say. It wasn't that easy to change things, as proved by the fact that it was midnight and she was out of bed pacing the room. She glanced at the huge, comfortable bed. There was nothing wrong with it, it was just too big for one person.

Luc's room was only a little way down the corridor.

That's a crazy idea, her sensible self warned.

Crazy or not, he had to get things off his chest.

Pardon me if I stay out of the way when he shoots you down in flames.

When you cared about someone that was a chance you had to take.

She smiled as she glanced at the door…the door she'd left a little bit open, as if Luc would take that sort of hint! He was far too worldly-wise to fall for her clumsy ruses these days. If he did notice her door was open, he'd close it as he walked past. Bottom line. If she didn't do something, nothing would change. Reviewing occasions of being proactive in the past, she could only conclude they'd all worked out well. There was no rule that said she had to wait around for things to happen, and she had no intention of revisiting that wallflower on the bench. It was time the wallflower took matters into her own hands. And there was no time like the present.

Sucking in a deep, steadying breath, she tiptoed out of the room. Padding down the corridor, as she had expected she found Luc's door firmly closed.

Turning the handle carefully, she opened the door without a noise. Cautiously peering in, she was rewarded by the sight of Lucas sprawled face down on the bed in all his naked splendour. She took a moment to admire him as she might admire a sculpture in a gallery. Built on a heroic scale, he was a magnificent sight.

She curbed a smile at the thought that her crazy plan was to slip into bed beside him. *And when he woke they'd have a chat?* Fantasies like that were dangerous. But how she longed for him…longed to feel his arms around her, and to make love quietly, deeply, tenderly—

In practical terms, there were two things wrong with that plan. She hadn't expected to find him naked or in full starfish position, so there wasn't an inch of bed to be had.

'Just leave, will you?'

She yelped with shock at the sound of his voice. 'I thought you were asleep.'

'Clearly not.' He shifted position, muscles rippling, but he kept his head turned away from her. 'I mean it, Stacey. Please leave. Now.'

She remained frozen in place by the door, trying to decide how best to rejig her plan. Slipping into bed beside him without waking him until they yawned, stretched, and reached for each other in the morning, according to the natural flow of things, clearly wasn't possible now.

Surprisingly, coming to a decision proved easier to navigate than she'd thought.

* * *

He'd heard her padding down the corridor, and was already on full alert when she entered the room. Having suspected something like this might happen, he hadn't even tried to sleep. She usually did as he asked in the end. That was his only comfort. Would she this time?

'I'm serious, Stacey. Say what you've got to say and then leave.'

In the shadows of the darkened room he couldn't see her expression clearly, and she remained silent, which forced him to prompt, 'Whatever it is you've got to say, just spit it out and go.'

'Make me.'

'I beg your pardon?'

'I'm not going anywhere unless you make me,' she said again.

'That's ridiculous.'

In the ghostly light her shoulders lifted and fell again. 'Ridiculous or not, I'm not going anywhere.'

'Until I eject you by force?'

'That's up to you.'

'This is wrong, Stacey. What happened between us in Barcelona was a mistake—'

'A mistake?' she interrupted in a voice full of raw wounds from the past. 'Is that what you think of me?'

'No,' he bit out. 'It's just that you don't belong here. I don't have anything to offer you, other than in a business sense, so please don't make this harder than it has to be.'

Undaunted, she walked towards the bed. Her face

was rigid and pale. But then, just as he should have expected, she firmed her jaw to confront him head-on. 'Isn't that for me to decide?' she asked. 'I know what I want, and I'm fully aware of what I'm doing.'

'You think you are,' he argued. 'But really, you've got no idea.'

'About you? I'd like to know you better, but you don't show yourself to anyone, do you, Luc? At least, I know some part of you,' she conceded, 'but that's only the part you've had the courage to show.'

'You're calling me a coward now?'

'I'm saying we're not so different. I don't find it any easier than you to show my feelings.'

'So you thought if we made love again it would all sort itself out?'

'I'm not that naïve. Pain that's taken years to build won't vanish with the first orgasm.'

Burying his hands in his hair, he said nothing.

'But if I've learned one thing, it's this,' she went on. 'If I want something, I know it won't fall into my lap. I have to get out there and make things happen.'

He raised his head. 'And that's what you're doing now?'

She smiled and shrugged.

'You're an intelligent and successful woman who has proved herself ten times over, which is exactly why you don't need me. There's no space for you in my life.'

'Nor you in mine,' she agreed. 'So must that consign us both to solitude for ever?'

What she was suggesting appeared to be a relationship of convenience, into which they would dip in and out as it suited them. Normally, he might applaud that sort of thing, but when Stacey was involved, the idea appalled him. He would not agree to flirting with her feelings. She'd get hurt.

Wouldn't he too?

So what? He doubted he was capable of feeling anything.

'Think what you like, but my answer's still no. I won't do anything to stop you moving forward.'

'Nice speech, but I'll stay here all night if I have to.'

'Please yourself,' he said, turning over in bed.

She didn't move.

'Go to bed, Stacey, before you get in any deeper.'

'But I want to be in deep. I want to experience life to the full. I *want* to feel. I don't want to be an onlooker. That only makes the ache inside me worse.'

'Oh, for goodness' sake!' Shooting up in bed, he glared at her.

She shrugged and smiled. 'There you are,' she whispered. 'Now, can I thank you for finding me?'

'You already did.'

'I don't mean when I was lost in the snow.'

'What do you mean?'

'Can I explain?' Before he could answer she was sitting on the bed. 'I just want to talk.'

Dipping his head, he gave her a disbelieving look. 'We can talk in the morning.'

'I don't want to wait that long.'

'Okay, so what do you want?'

'I want to have sex with you.'

His body responded immediately. 'Be very careful,' he warned.

'Why? Will you pounce on me?'

Swinging out of bed, he grabbed his jeans. 'Does this answer your question?'

'If you go you'll regret it.'

'I'll regret it if I don't go,' he assured her.

'Then, I guess it's up to me to stop you.'

'I'd like to see you try.'

Slipping off the bed, she knelt in front of him. 'Oh, I'm going to try all right,' she assured him.

Before he had the chance to stop her she drew her tee shirt over her head, revealing lush breasts. He could still remember the scent of them, and the taste of her skin. Her nipples were erect, and he grew harder in response. He didn't push her away; instead, he dragged her close. The ache, the need, the pain inside him could no longer be sustained.

'What the hell do you think you're doing now?' he asked sharply, throwing his head back to drag in some much-needed air as she made her intentions clear.

'Pleasuring you,' she informed him. 'Stay still, or I'll bite.'

Dios! What? The kitten had become a tigress. Lacing his fingers through her hair, he kept her close. A groan of pleasure escaped him. He needed this, needed Stacey, and she knew exactly what to do. Using her tongue, her teeth, and her lips, she made sure the outcome was inevitable. 'No!' he ex-

claimed at the very last minute. Control was everything. Here, in dodging the questions she asked him,
in business, in everything. Fisting his erection, he
pulled back.

Her eyes were wide and bewildered as she stared
up at him. 'Did I do something wrong?'

'You did nothing wrong. *This* is wrong. *We're*
wrong. This just cannot be.'

'Who says? We're not related. You're not very
much older than I am. Is it because I'm not rich, not
good enough for you? Or are you frightened of my
brother?'

'Your brother?' He shook his head and smiled.
'As for you not being good enough—'

'Don't bother,' she said, putting a crack in the
stone wall of his heart as she stumbled to her feet.
'I don't want to hear your excuses. I don't have the
patience to stick around while you find yourself.'

'Says you?' Grabbing her by the shoulders, he
brought her to her feet in front of him. 'Don't you
understand? I just can't think of you this way.'

'Still lying to yourself?' she countered tensely.
'Still hiding your feelings, Lucas? Is that why you've
got an erection? We're both consenting adults, and
however determined you are to banish emotion from
your life, you can't hide that.'

'Don't make this harder than it has to be.' He
stared pointedly at the door, but she refused to take
the hint, and instead made a cradle of her hands to
offer her breasts like a gift. This cut straight through
his desire to protect her from him, and made him

see the sensual woman he'd made love to in Barcelona. As if that weren't enough, she dipped down to capture his straining erection between her luscious curves.

'You like that, don't you?' she whispered. 'You don't want me to go now…'

As she began to move rhythmically to and fro, her question was redundant. Eventually, he managed to grind out, 'This does not mean I will allow you to seduce me.'

'Allow?' she said, angling her chin to one side as she stared up at him. 'I'd say you don't have any choice. Unless I decide otherwise, of course…'

CHAPTER NINE

SHE LET HIM go suddenly, which left him in an agony of frustration. Shaking his head, he barked an incredulous laugh at the incongruity of the situation. 'I suppose it's no use my telling you to go?'

'None at all,' she agreed.

'Then, for your sake, I must.'

'For my sake?' she said, moving quickly to stand between him and the door. 'If you were doing something for my sake you'd make love to me. You wouldn't walk out.'

'This is not a battle of wills,' he said, spearing a glance into her eyes as he fastened his jeans. 'It's about me caring for you.'

'Twaddle. It's about you reinforcing your barricades, leaving me feeling like a fool.'

Backing her into a shaft of moonlight that had unwittingly trespassed on the drama, he bit out, '*You* did nothing wrong. It's me. I'm wrong for you, and no amount of sex can make that right.'

'Try me,' she challenged.

He wanted to say a lot of things as he headed for the door, but prolonging this served no purpose.

Stacey flinched as the door closed behind Luc. Deep down she'd known this was a daft idea, and had been primed for disappointment. But she hadn't expected it to go quite so badly. Lucas was too sophisticated to fall for her clumsy ploys, and all she'd managed to prove tonight was that fantasies never played out as you expected them to. Only one thing was certain, and that was that she couldn't leave it here.

Scooping up her discarded pyjama top, she dressed and left the room. She found Luc downstairs in front of a guttering fire with shadows flickering around him, head back, eyes closed, jaw set, like a dark angel sitting on the steps of hell.

She wouldn't let him go through those gates. Somehow she was going to save him. And however *ridiculous* that sounded—a word he liked to use— she was a very determined woman.

He didn't say anything as she came closer, but she'd put money on him knowing she was there.

'Go away, Stace.'

'You haven't called me that for years.'

'I haven't *felt* this way for years.'

'Have you felt anything for years?'

Too deep, too intrusive a question, she thought when he remained silent. She tried again. 'How do you feel?'

'Conflicted,' he admitted. 'Contrary to what you

think, I want you more than you know, but if you expect hearts and flowers, you'll be disappointed.'

Of course she was disappointed. Didn't every woman want the dream? 'Did I say that was what I expect?'

'You didn't have to.'

Firming her jaw, she crossed the room and sat down on the sofa facing his.

'Believe me, Stace,' Luc said with a touch of warmth in his tone as he opened his eyes. 'You don't need me in your life.'

'Don't tell me what I need.'

'You have so little experience.'

'Of sex?' she queried. 'I'd agree with you where that's concerned, but I'm not inexperienced when it comes to life, and I know when someone's hurting.'

'That's your strength,' he agreed. 'One of them.'

'So...?'

'So, don't waste your time on me. I'm a lost cause, and there are plenty of people who could benefit from the kind of thoughtfulness and compassion you want to give.'

'You make me sound like a saint and I'm far from it.'

'Me too,' he confirmed dryly.

'Don't you think it's time to confront the demons from your past?'

'While I'm having sex with you?' he suggested in that same ironic tone.

Stacey shrugged. 'It's an outlet—yes.'

Luc's mouth tugged in a wry sort of smile. 'Who knows what you might release.'

'You, I hope,' she said. 'I do know that you'll continue to hurt until you allow yourself to feel something.'

'And I can't ask what you know about that, can I?'

'I don't pretend my situation was anything like yours,' she assured him. 'I can't even begin to imagine how you feel, but isn't that when we need our friends the most?'

'Friends?' he challenged. 'I thought we were talking about sex. That's certainly the impression you gave me upstairs.'

'Don't,' she said softly. 'I don't want to argue with you. I just want to help.'

'You always want to help.' Getting up, he stoked the fire. 'I don't need *help*, not from anyone, and especially not from you.'

Luc's words were like a slap across the face, and it took a little time before she could do much more than watch the flames rise and dance in the hearth.

'Okay,' she said at last, getting to her feet. 'I guess even I can take a hint.'

'Maybe we can talk some other time,' he suggested.

'Is there any point?'

'You were lucky tonight that it was me and not some other man,' Luc called after her as she headed for the stairs.

She stopped dead. 'There's no chance of there ever being another man.'

'Then, you're a fool, Stacey,' Luc said coldly. 'For

your own sake, accept that we don't belong together. You deserve someone far—'

'Oh, please,' she interrupted, 'spare me the gentle let-down. If I'm hopeless in bed and turn you right off, you only have to say so.'

'What the hell?' Luc was on his feet and grabbing hold of her within a second. Cupping her chin, he made her look at him. 'You're not hopeless. In fact, that's the problem.'

'I'm too good,' she suggested with a mocking huff as she braced to hear the truth.

'Yes,' Luc confirmed flatly. 'This is my fault. I shouldn't have let things go so far.'

'It takes two to tango. And as for consequences, I'll handle whatever comes around.'

'But can you do that?' His expression was sceptical. 'You're hunting for a fairy tale and what I'm looking for is sex. I devote most of my time to work and the rest of my time to polo. I travel constantly, and wherever I am—' he shrugged '—is home.'

'You don't have a home. You have a number of fabulous properties across the world, but when it comes to a home you don't know the meaning of the word.'

'I can remember,' he said quietly.

She could have ripped out her tongue. 'Of course you do. Luc, I'm so sorry. I don't think sometimes.'

'And you're not thinking now,' Luc warned.

'Oh, I am,' she assured him. 'What makes you think I want more than you? I'm a normal woman with normal, healthy appetites. Men aren't the only

animals on the planet who want sex with no consequences or long-term complications. I'm not
the clinging-vine type,' she added while her heart
screamed that she was a liar, and that she did want
Luc long-term. For as long as she could remember
he'd been part of her life, and life going forward
without him, especially now they'd been so close,
was unthinkable. But if one night was all she could
have she'd take it.

'Neither of us has the type of lifestyle that al-
lows for a long-term relationship,' she said matter-of-
factly, as desperation to have Luc kiss her, embrace
her, make love to her, drummed relentlessly in her
brain.

His lips pressed down attractively as he considered this. 'If you can accept reality, then I suppose...'

She jumped on the opening. 'Do you mean accepting the pace of your life means you snatch up a
woman like you snatch up a meal, and when you've
both had enough you walk away?'

Luc's head shot back. '*Dios*, Stacey! That's a little
harsh, even for me. I could never think of you that
way. I've watched you grow up.'

'Then you should know I'm no fool and I know
my own mind. Please don't pity me, or make a joke
of this, either. I know what I want, and I know what
you need. What's wrong with that?'

He shrugged. 'Everything?'

Cocking her chin to one side, she demanded,
'Doesn't that make it irresistible...for both of us?'

* * *

No. It did not. *Dios!* What was he going to do with this woman—with himself? The fire they created between them was unreal. One minute they were arguing, and the next passion of a very different kind was threatening. Any challenge, or something forbidden to him, had always proved irresistible in the past, but this was Stacey. This was wrong. With no reprieve in sight, the best he could do was put space between them. What a joke talking about consequences where Stacey was concerned. He'd taken her into his home and it was *he* who had to live with those consequences. According to the latest weather forecast it would be three or four days at least before the roads to the village were passable, so, like it or not, they were stuck together.

'Lucas?' she prompted. 'Don't you have anything to say?'

'Irresistible is a dangerous word.'

'Thank you for your input, Señor Da Silva. I shall bear that in mind.'

He had plenty more to say on the subject, but thought it better now to stare out of the window, beyond which snow was falling again. The hotel across the road had become a vague, insubstantial shadow, a reminder that he'd called every hotel in the village, but they were all full with people who'd been stranded. No one had any room for Stacey except him. 'Haven't you gone to bed yet?' he asked without turning to face her.

'I'm waiting for you,' she said.

When he swung around, she gave him one of her looks, and he knew then that even if they went to their separate beds she'd still be on his mind. 'You should rest and so should I.'

'I'll let you rest…in between making love to me.'

'This isn't funny, Stace.'

'You're telling me.'

To his horror, there were tears in her eyes. 'Just let it go,' he advised. 'I'm a lost cause,' he added wryly.

'Okay,' she agreed with a jerk of her head. 'That should be easy.' But instead of moving away, she moved closer. 'Wow. We really are snowed in…what a cliché. Now I have to share your bed.'

Not so much a cliché as a challenge, he thought as he attempted to ignore Stacey's appeal, her scent, her vulnerability. 'Your bed,' he emphasised.

'I can take a hint.'

He doubted it. 'Thanks for your help tonight.'

'I was pleased to help.'

They stood staring out at the snow, which had started banking up thanks to a strong wind, and was collecting in even deeper drifts around the chalet. He'd dig them out in the morning and ski her down to the lower part of the village, rather than sit around waiting for the weather to change. That was the safest thing to do, plus he had a party to think about. They both did. He laughed inwardly at the irony of trying to avoid someone for their own good, only to have fate bind them together.

'We're stranded on a desert island of snow,' Stacey murmured beside him.

'No more fantasies, please,' he begged.

Needless to say, she ignored him. 'It's like a different world, isn't it? No rules, and nothing beyond us and this moment.'

'It doesn't take long for your imagination to start rolling, does it?' he commented.

'Well, how do you see it?'

'As a task tomorrow morning when I dig us both out.'

'Practical to the last,' she remarked with a laugh.

'I'm practical,' he agreed. 'As you can be.'

'I do have some good qualities, then?'

'Stop fishing,' he warned, but she'd made him smile, which made him want her more than ever. He'd be the first to admit that years of guarding his siblings had made him overprotective. That was what his brothers and sister told him, anyway. 'You're no fun any more,' was a frequent complaint that he supposed might be true, but it hadn't stopped him enjoying Stacey.

Did he really have to stop?

For her sake, yes.

'It's beautiful, isn't it?' she whispered, and then he felt her hand on his back… Her tiny hand on flesh he hadn't troubled to cover since leaving his bed. The sensation was incredible. 'Get out of here,' he said lightly, hoping she would, because his willpower had taken just about all it could.

'No,' she said flatly, and, rather than obey him,

she ran the tips of her nails down his supersensitive skin, sending his moral compass into a spin.

Swinging around, he stared at her. 'No?' he queried.

She glanced down. Instantly hard, he was incapable of hiding his physical reactions; thoughts were much easier.

They stared at each other for a good few moments, then he reached out to hook his fingers into the waistband of her pyjamas. As he pulled them down he observed, 'So you're not entirely made of ice.'

'Try me,' he suggested.

'I intend to.'

A cry of triumph shot from her throat as he knelt between her thighs.

'Oh…please,' she begged as he began to explore her body as if he had never encountered it before. By bending her knees she increased the pressure from his tongue. Working her hips to and fro lazily, she was all too soon wailing, 'I can't hold on.'

'You're not supposed to, princess.'

And then she screamed out wildly, *'Yes! Yes… Yes!'* before exhaling noisily in time to each violent spasm as it washed over her.

'Oh, Lucas,' she moaned contentedly when the pleasure began to fade. 'That was amazing.'

Catching her as she collapsed, sated for the moment, he knew he had never wanted a woman more, had never wanted to pleasure a woman more. With all the barriers finally removed between them he swung her into his arms, and carried her to the deep fur rug in front of the fire. Arranging her to his liking, he parted her legs wide and allowed them to rest on his shoulders as he dipped his head and parted her lips to lave her with his tongue.

'I can't—not again—not so soon,' she insisted on a gasping breath.

'And I say you can,' he argued quietly, 'and not once, but many times.'

He proved it by delicately agitating the tiny bud at the heart of her pleasure. It didn't take much encouragement for it to spring back to life.

Exhaling with excitement, Stacey wound her fingers through his hair to keep him close. He knew what she wanted, and he gave it to her until she was thrusting her hips towards him, crying out, 'More… *More!* Don't stop!' Seconds later, she called out his name and fell noisily into release.

He held her firmly in place to make sure that she enjoyed every last pulse of pleasure. 'I had no idea it could be so good,' she groaned when the initial violence of her climax had begun to subside into a series of rhythmical pulses.

That was the problem, he reflected as he gradually brought her down again with soothing words in his own language and long, gentle strokes of his hand. Stacey was beginning to understand what was possible, and from there it was only a small step to feral lust, and when that point was reached, there'd be no turning back.

What was he talking about? They'd already

crossed the Rubicon, he realised as she gripped his arms fiercely to state baldly, 'I want you inside me.'

She had no idea how much he wanted her closing around him, holding him in place as she drew him deep and sucked him dry. 'Please,' she whispered, 'tease me like you did before.'

Reaching for his belt, she unbuckled it and snapped it out of its loops. Then she popped the button at the top of his zipper. The moment that came down he exploded out of the placket.

'Is this what you want?' he asked, bracing himself above her.

'Exactly that,' she agreed.

'Like this,' he suggested, stroking the tip of his erection down the apex of her thighs.

'Oh, yes,' she confirmed.

'And this?' he suggested, watching her closely as he gave her the tip.

'Oh, yes…yes, *yes*!'

Capturing her wrists in one fist, he pinned them above her head. 'Just one thing…'

'What?' she gasped.

'I say we take this slowly.'

'At first,' she agreed.

CHAPTER TEN

FANTASIES ABOUT MASTERFUL Lucas were nothing compared to this. She could dream of making love until the lights went out and the world ended and this would still be on another scale.

Luc was so much more than she remembered. That first time was nothing like this, because now she was ready and she welcomed his size and the way he stretched her. All her inhibitions had dropped away, so by the time he had protected them both, pressed her down and taken her as firmly as she could have wished, she was ready to respond with matching fire.

She'd dreamed for so long that one day Lucas would see her as a woman, rather than as an annoying nuisance who cropped up in his life now and then, that she refused to be responsible for the sounds and words leaving her throat. They were wild for each other. And while she was consumed by a ravenous hunger, the urge to be one with him was even stronger.

She was eager for more, but Luc refused to be

hurried. He would take care of her, he insisted as he began a leisurely tour of her body that required him to kiss every part of her.

'Stop, stop,' she begged when he nuzzled the sensitive nape of her neck with his sharp black stubble. Sensation overload. 'I can't stand it,' she gasped out, thrashing about.

'But you can,' he said.

Turning her, he proved this by kissing the back of her knees, where she hadn't even known she was sensitive, and then he kissed his way up her thighs, and on across her buttocks until she was trembling with anticipation. Next, he kissed the sway of her back until she groaned with contentment. He knew what he was doing. With every passing second she was becoming more sensitive. Her pulse was going crazy and her body craved him like never before.

'Again?' he suggested.

She smiled up as he eased her legs apart and moved between them. Grasping his erection, he teased her with the tip.

'Yes! *Yes!*' she groaned, arcing her hips instinctively to receive him. 'Don't stop now,' she begged. 'Don't you dare stop.'

And to some extent, he obeyed her, stroking and teasing as before, then entering a little way before pulling back again. It was a game she loved. Their game.

Grabbing Luc's shoulders, she drew her knees back and took the chance, brief as it was, to admire the magnificent power of the body looming over her.

He was so careful with her, sinking a little deeper each time, until finally he was engaged to the hilt.

'Soon,' he murmured in reply to her gasping protests when he stopped moving.

'You okay?' he asked as she gasped with pleasure.

She couldn't speak for fear of breaking the spell. They were one, and that was all she cared about.

Dropping kisses on her lips, he began to move, not back and forth as he had before, but in a circular, massaging movement until her body could do nothing but respond. 'Oh!' she cried out in wonder as she drew closer to the abyss. *'Again...!'*

Luc obliged by slamming into her, so that this time when the waves hit they were stronger and fiercer, and what was almost better than that was when she closed her inner muscles around him and he groaned. Seeing him lost in pleasure of her making made her feel powerful and strong, while the discovery that by tensing and relaxing her inner muscles she could bring him pleasure thrilled her beyond belief.

They made love in front of the fire for hours, fiercely at first, and then tenderly, which she found almost unbearably poignant. When Lucas brushed her hair back from her glowing face, she knew without question that if nothing good ever happened again she'd cling to tonight and never forget it. What more could she want than this closeness, this oneness as they stared deep into each other's eyes? It required a special sort of trust to give herself to a man so completely.

'I don't know if you want to sleep, but I think you will sleep now,' Luc observed, smiling down. 'It's been a long day. You must be exhausted.'

'And a very long night,' she reminded him, 'though, surprisingly, I don't feel tired at all. You, on the other hand, must be exhausted?'

'I've never worked so hard,' he agreed dryly, grinning with pleasure as she tightened her muscles around him. 'Always a contest with you,' he added as she enticed him to do more than drop kisses on her lips.

They breathed in unison, with every part of them in full accord, and every part of their naked bodies touching. She'd never felt so safe, so cared for...*so loved?*

No. Don't kid yourself like that, Stacey's inner voice recommended. *It's too cruel. You won't be able to bear it in the morning when you see everything through the lens of a bright new day.*

'I'd like to go to bed and sleep in your arms,' she said honestly.

'Sleep?' Lucas queried.

'Yes. Sleep,' she confirmed. 'For whatever remains of the night.'

'Not much,' he observed with a glance out of the window to where dawn's first frail rays were already silvering the mountain peaks.

'Whatever's left of the night, I'll take it.'

Luc's answer was to lift her into his arms so he could carry her to the bed.

There was no greater peace, he mused as he

watched Stacey sleeping. No greater satisfaction than making love to a woman that he...

That he what?

Loved? Cherished? Had used?

Not used. Never used.

They'd come together because, short of swearing a vow of chastity, there was no other way for them. It was inevitable, and had always been inevitable since the first moment they met. Stacey had imprinted her unique and infuriating qualities on him in a way he couldn't have imagined possible, and now could never forget. She'd slept in his arms, giving him the gift of peace for the first time in years. Her breathing, so gentle and even, had soothed his. She looked so innocent and that soothed him too. He needed some uncomplicated goodness in his life, but that was selfish when he had nothing to offer Stacey long-term. It would be disingenuous to say he regretted that his darker side ruled his caring instinct. When she woke, Stacey would surely have come to her senses, and know that what they'd shared was over.

Even an ice-cold shower failed to subdue his libido. He'd never known another woman like her. Stacey had been wild when she was younger, but in his bed she'd been a revelation. Niahl's little sister was all grown up. Still cloaked in innocence perhaps, but beneath that cloak her sexual appetite matched his.

And Niahl? How would he square this with Niahl? This need, this lust inside him blurred the edges of right and wrong, making it hard to move on. The bottom line didn't include Niahl, he determined as he turned off the water and shook hair out of his eyes. The bottom line was Stacey. He didn't want to hurt her. Reaching for a towel, he secured it around his waist. He only had to think of her and he was hard.

Dropping the towel, he glanced out of the window at snow banked up high in drifts. *Avoid her if you can*, his inner critic challenged. He and Stacey had been thrown together and now they were stranded together. The only sensible answer to that problem was to clear a path in the snow to the black slope and ski her back to the village.

Donning work clothes, he congratulated himself on the fact that he'd always been able to identify the right moment to part. He'd known with his siblings when it was time for them to leave home, and he knew with Stacey. She needed a man who would have time for her, and dote on her, and provide her with a safe and cosy home. History suggested he could never do that. As soon as his siblings were fledged, he'd cast off, a ship without an anchor. After his parents' death nothing had remained the same. Life was a river continually moving on. This chalet wasn't his home. Stacey was right. It was just one of many properties he owned across the world. The next acquisition was always more attractive. And in each there was something vital missing. If he could just put his finger on what it was…he'd buy it, Luc concluded as he headed downstairs.

* * *

Stacey woke in a state of deep contentment, instantly aware of a body well used. It took her a moment longer to realise where she was. *Luc's room!* And then the events of the previous night came flooding in. Reaching out to touch him in the big, wide bed, she found the other side empty. Where was he?

'Luc...?'

The silence that greeted her question had a particular quality that told her she was alone. Slipping out of bed, she grabbed a robe. Putting it on, she belted it. Crossing to the window, she exclaimed softly with relief to see Luc outside, clearing a path through the snow. Turning, she retired to the bathroom, where she took the fastest shower ever. She frowned as she put on the only clothes she had with her. There was a suspicion tugging at the back of her mind.

She'd examine it later, she decided as she hurried downstairs to put on her jacket and boots. There were all sorts of useful implements hanging on the wall of the boot room alongside the skis, so she grabbed a shovel and went outside to join him.

'Morning...'

'Hey.' Luc glanced up briefly before stabbing his shovel back in the snow.

She could feel his eyes burning beneath wraparound sunglasses—a necessary precaution when the sun was low and bright. Whether the sky would remain blue like this remained to be seen, but while it did...

'Shot!' She'd got him square on the head with a snowball.

Shaking his unruly mop of black hair like an irritated wolf, Luc dug his shovel into the snow again and acted as if he hadn't noticed.

She tried again, and then again with mounting success, until, with a roar, he straightened up.

'You don't frighten me, Luc Da Silva,' she assured him.

'Then it's time I did,' he said, and in a couple of strides he was transformed from cool and aloof to the infuriating guy she remembered from her youth. Yanking her close, he plonked her down and dropped great handfuls of snow on her face, rubbing still more into her hair.

'Don't you—'

'Dare?' he suggested. '*Dios*, Stacey! You make me want to have you right here in the snow.'

'I don't see anyone stopping you…'

With a husky exclamation, he tossed his gloves aside. 'What are you doing to me?'

'And you to me,' she gasped as they began to fight with each other's clothes.

'Is this even possible?' Thermals stood in their way.

'Of course,' Luc confirmed as he freed himself.

Swinging her up so she could wrap her legs around his waist, he took her with a deep thrust. No foreplay, none needed. An exclamation of shocked delight flew from her throat. Nothing had ever felt this good. She was more than ready for him, and

Luc was so caring, so careful of his size and her much smaller body. He held her as if she weighed nothing, and pounded into her until she could do no more than hang suspended in his arms. 'So good... I need this...'

'Me too,' Lucas admitted in an edgy growl.

'Harder! Faster!' They were wild for each other. She couldn't get enough. How could she ever live without this...without him?

'Again,' she insisted throatily when the first bout of pleasure started to fade. 'I need more.'

Luc laughed. 'Me too,' he assured her.

'Yes!' she hissed in triumph as he thrust rhythmically the way she liked.

'How strong are you?' she said some time later. 'Don't your arms ache?'

'I hadn't even thought about it. I was somewhat distracted.'

'And now?'

'And now...I want to have you in the snow.'

Beneath a bright blue sky with snow hillocks all around them, they made love again, and this time when Luc pinned her arms above her head, they stared into each other's eyes, and saw more than the fever of passion.

'I guess we'd better get to work,' he said reluctantly some time later.

'I guess we better had,' she agreed.

Arranging their clothes took less than a few seconds, and soon they were attacking the snow with real gusto.

'Something wrong?' she asked Luc, shooting a glance his way when he stopped shovelling and leaned on the handle. 'Have I exhausted you?'

He huffed a laugh and gathered her close. 'What do you think?'

'I think you're facing a decision between clearing the path, and visiting that sauna over there.'

'Could be,' he confirmed with a grin.

'Let's investigate. I don't want to leave you in agony.'

Planting their shovels, they ran to the sauna. Closing the door, they stripped off each other's clothes. The small log cabin was already warm, but Luc raised the temperature even more, both with water on the embers and with his unique take on lovemaking on scorching wooden benches. 'We have to be quick,' he explained, laughing against her mouth.

'I can be quick.'

'When you want to,' he agreed.

'I like to make you work.'

'I noticed.'

His grin was infectious, a slash of strong white teeth against his deep tan and sharp black stubble. There was only one problem. Their enthusiasm combined with the extreme heat inside the sauna sent the logistics of sex haywire. 'I'm sliding off you!'

'Time to cool down,' Luc agreed.

Who knew they could be so close? There was a lot of laughter involved as he carried her outside and dumped her in the snow, where they proved conclusively that heating up before rolling in ice crystals was a great aphrodisiac. Luc's strength and potency was glaring her in the face. His naked body, challenging the elements, had never looked more magnificent. 'On top of me,' he instructed, arranging her so she could mount him. 'Can't risk you catching cold.'

'No chance of that!' She gasped out her pleasure as he entered her in one thrust, and when she was quiet again and snuggled into his chest, she remarked groggily, 'No wonder this caught on.'

'Making love in the snow?'

'The whole sauna thing.' Had they ever been so close? she wondered.

'Come on.' Luc dragged her to her feet. 'Before we both freeze. Heat. Clothes. Then back to work.'

They talked as they worked, giving her hope that Luc might finally open up. He didn't. Instead he directed a barrage of questions her way, so she told him about her life and friends in London, and the fact that she missed the farm. 'I miss the horses terribly,' she admitted. 'And I miss Niahl, but he's so busy these days.' She stopped as a shadow crossed Luc's face. *Luc* was so busy these days. This snow-bound interlude was a rare break for him. *That* was what he'd been trying to tell her, that she shouldn't expect anything beyond this, because he didn't have the time. That was okay. On the personal front, she could deal with it. She'd have to. But where Luc was concerned, if she could unlock even just a little bit of his angst, her job was done, and so she asked the question: 'How about you, Lucas?'

'Me?' His lips pressed down as he shrugged. 'You

can learn anything you want to know about me from the press.'

'Can I?' she said disbelievingly. 'I can only learn what sensational journalism wants me to know, and I'd rather hear it from you.'

'Hear what from me?'

Okay. She got the message. This was going nowhere. If she pressed him he'd clam up even more. Why spoil the short time they had together?

'No.' Planting her shovel, she admitted, 'Whatever I read in the press, I see you as amazing. Always have.' She huffed a laugh. 'Pity me.'

'No faults?' Luc enquired, spreading his arms wide.

Stacey hummed as she pretended to consider this, but she was thinking, *This is my chance to let Luc know I'm there for him.*

'You're a little controlling, but only because responsibility came along in such a tragic way. However wild you were, there was no option but to rein in fast. Perhaps you overcompensated. Your parents' death happened when others your age were free to do as they pleased, so I think it's amazing that you not only built a business empire, but mended a family that had been so badly fractured.'

What she didn't add was her deeply held belief that Luc could have done with someone to mend him.

He hummed and raised a brow. 'I'm not sure I deserve that level of praise. You make me sound far more impressive than I am.'

'Do I?' She held his gaze steadily. 'Or do I say these things because they're true?'

'You haven't done too badly yourself,' he said, shifting the spotlight with effortless ease. 'You were also bound by duty, but you found an opportunity to try something new and forge your own path, which you've done very successfully, it seems to me.'

Disappointment welled inside her. She should have known better than to expect Luc to open up after so many years for no better reason than because she'd asked a question. Deciding to keep things light and try another time, she smiled. 'So you've finally accepted I've changed in five years.'

'I wouldn't go that far,' he growled, pretending to be fierce.

'Just a little?' she suggested.

He dragged her close. 'Quite a lot. Seems to me you've grown up in a very short time.'

'Are you surprised?' she said softly, smiling happily against his mouth. 'One night with you is enough to make anyone grow up. My initiation ceremony was spectacular. I can't recommend it enough.'

'I suggest you keep it to yourself.'

'Oh, I will,' she promised fervently. 'And please don't let this be the last time,' she whispered before she could stop herself.

'Let's finish the dig,' he said, easing out of their embrace.

'We'll feel much better for completing the task,' she said, packing away her feelings.

'Time will tell,' Luc agreed.

'And when time has done its job?'

He shrugged. 'We'll know.'

She didn't ask him what they'd know. The answer was clear to both of them. Time would push them apart, but there was no point in thinking about that now.

CHAPTER ELEVEN

THEY MET UP in the great room, having taken a shower after their marathon snow-shovelling endeavours. 'You look great,' Luc told her with a wicked smile. 'Exercise suits you.'

'You too,' she said a little distractedly, though Luc had never looked better than he did right now. Barefoot in a pair of old jeans, unshaven with his thick, wavy hair damp and clinging to his stubble, powerful torso clad in a faded tee shirt that had definitely seen better days, he could play the role of gypsy king to perfection. A very handsome, rugged, and extremely virile gypsy king, she amended as their stares clashed and locked.

'You've changed,' he said, frowning.

'For the better, I hope?'

'Hmm. I can't quite put my finger on it.'

But she could. He was right saying she'd changed. She'd changed more than he knew. She was late and she was never late. And there was more evidence that she might be pregnant, though this was something that other people might find hard to believe. Call it instinct, but she felt very different in a deep and fundamental way. She was as sure as she could be that she was no longer alone in her body, but was the nurturing home of a new young life. Her heart had expanded to embrace this new love, though where she went from here remained a mystery. She could only be confident about one thing, and that was that she would approach everything as she always did, head-on. She didn't sit on those thoughts, but came straight out with them. 'What if I seem different to you because I'm pregnant?'

Lucas stilled. 'I'm sorry? What did you say?'

'What if I'm pregnant?' she repeated. 'What if I'm having your baby?'

'That isn't possible.' Luc shook his head confidently. 'I made sure of it.'

'No one can make absolutely sure of that, not even you, Luc.'

'All right,' he conceded grudgingly. 'So how can you be absolutely sure that you are pregnant without undergoing the usual tests?'

'I'm as sure as I can be. It can happen the first time you make love.'

Luc frowned. 'Barcelona?'

'Almost a month ago,' she confirmed.

Thoughts flickered fast behind his eyes, and she was sure those thoughts said that a child didn't figure on Luc's agenda. He didn't even think of her long-term, let alone a child. So? So she'd manage on her own. She'd done it before and she'd do it again. She wouldn't be the only single mother in the world.

And one thing was certain, no baby of hers would suffer rejection as she had. It would be loved unconditionally. A career and motherhood were compatible. It would take some organising, but she was good at that—

'Stacey? You do know we can't leave this here?'

'Of course I do.'

'Then…?'

'May I make a suggestion?'

'Of course.'

They had both turned stiff and businesslike. Pushing away regret and every other emotion, she concentrated on the facts. 'Let's wait until we're no longer snowbound and I can have a test. Then get the party out of the way before we discuss the particulars.'

'The *particulars*?' Lucas drew his head back with surprise. 'We *are* still talking about a child?'

Stacey's face flamed red. Of course they were. The expression in Luc's eyes shamed her. It was that of a man who had only ever known love from his parents, and who couldn't fathom Stacey's deeply held fear. Not having known her own mother, she worried that she might know nothing about mothering and mess up. It wouldn't be for want of trying. Now the seed of suspicion was planted in her brain, she wanted to be pregnant, already loved the thought of a child with all her heart.

'We're discussing the most precious gift in the world,' she stated firmly. Whatever else he thought of her, she couldn't bear to have Luc think she took after her father.

'Come here,' he murmured.

She hesitated, knowing that with each show of affection it was harder to accept that they couldn't do this together. Luc had no reason to change his life. Just as she wouldn't be the first single mother, he wouldn't be the first man with a love child, but that didn't mean they would become a family.

But she did go to him. And they did kiss. Enveloping her in a tender bear hug as if she were suddenly made of rice paper, he whispered against her hair, 'I shouldn't have let you dig the snow.'

She gazed up. 'I might be pregnant, but I'm not sick, and I'd like to have seen you stop me.'

'Still,' he said in a serious tone, pulling back to stare into her face. 'Take it easy from now on until you know.'

When people cared for her it brought tears to her eyes. Having Luc care for her was catastrophic, and these were tears she could do without, so she turned away before he'd seen them, in case he thought her weak.

'I've not finished with you yet,' he murmured.

The tone of his voice made her look at him. He pulled her close. Their mouths collided. They kissed as if tomorrow would never come.

Luc took some time for reflection alone in his study while Maria prepared a light lunch for him and Stacey. His experience of family life had been positive until the accident, when he had vowed never to risk his heart again. The pain of losing his parents had been indescribable. It still was. The wound cut deep and he had thought himself incapable of loving again.

A child changed everything.

Now he'd have to risk his heart. Anticipation and dread fought inside him at the thought. Where was he supposed to find time in his busy schedule for a child? Would he be any use as a father? He'd been lucky enough to have brilliant parents. Love had been in full supply, though their grasp of life and economics had been sadly lacking, as he had discovered when he took over the responsibility of running the family home. These days he could mastermind the biggest deals, and buy anything he wanted, but he still remembered the restrictions placed on him when he was caring for his brothers and sisters. It was a responsibility he'd taken on gladly, but he couldn't deny it was a relief when they were old enough to make their own way in life. Of course, they didn't know yet if Stacey was pregnant, but if she was, with her background, she'd need support too. He'd make time, Luc concluded.

First things first. For Stacey's peace of mind, he had to get her down to the village where she could take a pregnancy test, see a doctor, and get up to speed with the arrangements for the party. She'd start climbing the walls if she couldn't do that soon. With transport to the village suspended there was only one way to get her down safely, and he was confident he could do it. He wouldn't take risks with Stacey. The thought of anything happening to her—

Nothing would happen to her. He must put the

past behind him. There were more important things to consider. His parents' death had been a tragic accident. That was what the police had told him afterwards, and only he knew the truth. Nothing Stacey could say or do would deter him from caring for her. And, if she proved to be pregnant, caring for their child. It was a surprise, but a good surprise, he reflected with a smile. They had certainly put enough work into it! He'd taken precautions, but precautions were never guaranteed one hundred per cent. So his duty now was to take care of her…and, quite incredibly, but undeniably possible, his unborn child. Whatever else happened from here on in he was determined that their baby, if there proved to be one, would know the loving upbringing he'd had, and not the tragically lonely home life that Stacey had known.

Decision made, he called Maria on the house phone. 'Hold lunch. I'm going to ski down to the village to check on the arrangements for the party.'

'Will Señorita Winner stay here?'

'Señorita Winner is coming with me.'

'No way!' Stacey exclaimed when Luc told her what he planned. 'Are you kidding me?'

'Don't you trust me?'

'You know I do.'

'But…?' he prompted.

'But if I'm pregnant…'

'You're not sick, as you put it,' he reminded her, 'and there's a smaller risk of having an accident if

I take you back to the village, than if I leave you to your own devices up here. The frustration of not knowing where the plans are for the party will kill you…if the roof doesn't cave in from the weight of snow first.'

She glanced up to the exposed rafters with concern. 'Is there a danger of that?'

'No,' Luc admitted. 'But for the sake of the party and my guests, as well as getting you checked out, we need to get down to the village asap. The gondolas aren't running yet, so what I'm proposing is the safest way.'

'You're that good a skier? Of course you are,' she commented dryly. 'Is there anything you can't do?'

'I don't know.' He shrugged. 'Let's find out. You haven't eaten anything, so I'll take you for lunch.'

Stacey's eyes widened. 'Let me get this straight. You're proposing to take me to the village on *your* skis?'

'On my skis,' Luc confirmed.

'You are joking, I hope?' Stacey stared down the dizzying drop. 'This is a cliff edge. You can't possibly ski down it.'

She let out a yelp as Luc proved her wrong. With his arm locked around her waist, he kept her securely in place on the front of his skis as he dropped from the edge like a stone. Just when she thought they would continue like that to the bottom of the mountain, he made a big sweeping turn, before heading sideways at a much slower pace, until finally he stopped at the side of the slope. 'See? I told you that you can trust me to keep you safe.'

'Just warn me when you're going to do something like that again,' she begged through ice-cold lips.

'I won't let you fall,' he promised. 'I could lift you off the ground in front of me and still take us both down the mountain safely, but if you stand on my skis it's easier for me to put my arms around you to keep you in place.'

'I wish you joy of that,' she said, laughing tensely at her hopeless joke.

'True,' Lucas agreed. His lips pressed down attractively. 'I've been trying to keep you in place for years and haven't succeeded, so I have no idea what makes me think I can do it now.'

'You trust me?' she suggested.

He huffed a laugh, then coaxed, 'Come on. Let's try another run. Just a short one until you get used to it.'

'Won't my boots crack your skis?'

'You're wearing snow boots, and you've only got little feet.'

'You've got slim skis,' she pointed out.

'But big feet,' Luc countered.

'Very big feet,' she agreed, tensing as they started to move again.

Stacey's throat dried as she stared down the abyss. Her job had taken her to some surprising places, but nothing like this. Only desperation to know if she was pregnant, and to see the team again so she could get the final plans for the party under way, could make her grit her teeth and carry on. Was this her preferred method of descending a mountain? If Luc hadn't been involved, her answer would be a firm no.

Nothing about being with Lucas is normal. Get used to it, her inner voice advised.

And she did. After the first few frightening drops, shimmies and turns, Luc tracked across the entire width of the slope, before stopping to make sure she was okay to continue. 'Enjoy it,' he urged. 'This is the closest you'll come to flight without leaving the ground.'

She forced a laugh. 'Please don't leave the ground. I saw those drops from the gondola before the storm closed in.'

'Don't worry. I ski this slope several times a day when I'm here, so I know it like the back of my hand.'

'How often do you look at the back of your hand?'

He laughed and they were off again, though not straight down as she had feared, but swooping from side to side in a rhythmical pattern she could almost get used to, if she could only close her mind to the fear of what seemed to her to be a controlled fall down the mountain.

'Relax,' Luc murmured against her cheek the next time he brought them to a halt. His mouth was so close they shared the same crisp champagne air.

'I want to trust you. Honestly I do. I trusted you with my body, so it should only be a small step to trust you with my life, shouldn't it?' Her laugh sounded tense, even to her, and Luc's expression was unreadable.

'There are no small steps up here,' she observed with a twist of her mouth. 'It's all giant leaps and furious speed, and I don't get how you do it while I'm standing on the front of your skis. It's a miracle I don't quite believe in yet.'

'Just believe I'll keep you safe. That's all you need to do,' Luc told her with an easy shrug. And with that they were off again, skimming down the slope.

Surprising herself, Stacey found her confidence gradually growing as she got used to the speed. It helped that Luc made regular stops 'to check she was still breathing', as he jokingly put it.

'I'm tougher than I look,' she assured him.

'No mistaking that,' he said.

No mistake at all. With Luc's body moulded tightly to hers, she wasn't skiing, she was flying, and with the wind in her face and his heat behind her, the experience was wonderful, magical. There was silence all around, apart from the swish of skis on snow, and not one other person on the mountain to disturb the solitude. It was just the two of them, equally dependent on the cooperation of the other. 'I can see the houses in the village,' she called out at last.

Luc cruised to a halt. The mist had cleared, and the snow had stopped falling, leaving the sky above an improbable shade of unrelieved blue. 'Suddenly, I feel optimistic,' she exclaimed excitedly, turning to look at him.

'Me too,' Luc agreed in more considered tone. 'This is perfect weather for the party.'

The party. Something went flat inside her. She didn't want to be reminded that her whole purpose in being here was to arrange a party for Luc. But those were the bald facts. He was thinking ahead, while she was guilty of living in the moment.

'If only the gondolas were running,' she remarked, staring up in a failed attempt to distract herself from the hurt inside her. They were halfway down the mountain, but there was no sign of any small cabins bobbing along. 'I would have thought that with the return of reasonably good weather they'd be running by now.'

'Wind damage,' Luc explained, following her gaze before tightening his grip around her waist and setting off again. 'Each part of the system will have to be thoroughly checked before they're operational,' he yelled in her ear.

'But your guests…'

'Don't worry,' he shouted back. 'I've got an idea to transport them up the mountain.'

'I'm intrigued.'

'And I'm hungry. Are you up for going a bit faster with no stops until we reach the village?'

'Yes!' Stacey surprised herself with how much she wanted this. Testing herself with Luc at her back was easy. She felt so safe with him, and happier than she had been in a long time. Whatever the future held they'd have much to celebrate. And if that future didn't promise to be exactly conventional, the prospect of maybe having a child to crown that happiness was a precious gift she looked forward to, no matter what.

There was no point thinking *if only*, Luc reflected as he slowed at the approach to the nursery slopes bordering the village. He'd done too much of that. *If only* his parents had lived to see how successful his brothers and sister had become. *If only* they could share his good fortune. And now, *if only* they had lived to see their first grandchild. Wherever he was in life, and whatever the circumstances, the guilt he bore sat on his shoulder like an ugly crow waiting to peck out his happiness.

Stacey whooped with exhilaration as he slowed to a stop, then she noticed his expression and asked with concern, 'You okay?'

'Me? Fine.'

'That's my line,' she scolded.

He huffed a laugh that held no humour. Steadying her as she stepped off his skis, he freed the bindings, stepped out of them, paired the skis, and swung them over his shoulder.

As she glanced back up the mountain and shook her head in wonder at what she'd accomplished, he remarked, 'If I told you at the top that we were about to ski the World Cup course, would you have come with me?'

Her jaw dropped as she stared at him. 'Really?'

'Really,' he confirmed. 'Well done.'

She grinned. 'Maybe not,' she admitted, 'but I'm

glad I did. You never had any doubt we'd get down safely, did you?'

'If I had you wouldn't be here. I would never take risks with your safety, especially not now. Anyway, congratulations again. You can tell your friends what you've done.'

Oddly, she felt flat. Maybe because Luc had made it sound like a holiday adventure, Stacey reflected as they walked along. Perhaps that was all it was to him. It made her wonder if the possibility that she might be pregnant had made any impact on him. Was he really so unfeeling, and if so why? Once the party was over they would speed off in opposite directions. Would Luc keep her at a distance? Surely a child was an everlasting link between them? Whether he wanted that link, however, was another matter. She trusted him completely, and yet she didn't know him at all, Stacey concluded as they walked along. As always, her concern for Luc won through over any other concerns she might have had. 'How will you get back to the chalet when you've finished your business in the village?'

'I won't be going back to the chalet.'

'Oh… I see.' She didn't see, but Luc didn't offer any more information, and she didn't feel it was her place to cross-question him. The last thing she wanted was for him to think her a clinging vine before she even knew if she was pregnant.

Everything about him suggested Luc was back in work mode. As she should be, Stacey reminded herself. They weren't lovers of long standing, let alone close friends, and when it came to his party in the mountains Lucas was the boss and she worked for him. She'd always known this had to end at some point. She just hadn't expected it to end so abruptly at the bottom of a ski slope after such an amazing run, when she'd been so sure the shared experience had brought them closer.

'I might stay over in the village,' he revealed in an offhand tone.

There was no invitation to join him, and why should there be? That said, it didn't make it any easier to accept how loving and caring he could be one minute, and how distant the next.

Of course you understand why he's this way, her inner voice insisted. The ability to love had died inside Luc on the day his parents were killed. Everyone but Niahl and Stacey had been surprised by the intensity of his grief. It had almost seemed Luc held himself responsible for his parents' death, but they'd been such a close family, loving and caring for each other, no wonder he'd been devastated. Many times she'd longed to tell him that he couldn't be everywhere at once, working up a business, and caring for parents who, however lovely they'd been, had struck Stacey as being unrealistic, even irresponsible, when it came to money. They were always chasing the next new idea, leaving Luc to bail them out on many occasions. The true extent of their debt had only come to light after the funeral, which Stacey believed had been the driver for Luc believing it was down to him to support his siblings and to pay off those debts. He had nothing to regret, and she only wished she could tell him so, but doubted in his present mood he'd appreciate it.

She flashed up a glance into his harsh, unyielding face. Loving might be beyond Luc, but caring was instinctive, having been bred into him by those same wacky, but deeply loving parents. He'd done so much for her already, she mused as they crossed the road, giving her confidence she'd never had in her body, and a sense of being wanted, which was entirely new. For however short a time, he'd made her believe she was worth wanting, and if whatever it was they had between them ended today, she would always be grateful for what Luc had taught her. Now it was up to her to accept this short time together for what it was: a brief reunion; amazing sex; care for each other and a renewal of friendship, as well as all the support she could wish for when it came to personal concerns, as well as in her professional life. It would be a mistake to read more into it. Luc was a realist, she was a dreamer, and if she mixed up the two she'd be heading for disappointment.

'We'll have lunch here,' Luc said as they approached a busy café with steamed-up windows. 'Then you can call by the pharmacy on your way to meet up with your team, and book an appointment with the local doctor for a check-up.'

He barely drew breath before adding, 'I'll speak

to my people, while you see yours, and then we'll
have a joint meeting.'

To discuss the party, and clearly not the results
of a pregnancy test or her visit to the local doctor.
Shouldn't they be discussing their future?

Their future? *Touch base with reality*, Stacey's
inner voice recommended.

Luc's only interest at this precise moment was
the vastly elaborate and hugely expensive party he'd
paid for. Other things could wait. That was how he
operated. Luc prioritised. He was a process-driven
man. She was the dreamer, or had she forgotten
that?

'Of course,' she confirmed in the same businesslike tone. She had filled a space in Luc's life, and
now he was done with her. 'Actually, I'd like to eat
with my team, if that's okay with you?'

He looked at her with surprise. 'Whatever you
want.'

'Forgive me—and thank you for your hospitality—
but I've been away long enough.' One sweeping ebony
brow lifted as Luc stared at her and frowned. 'Everything should be ready for the party,' she hurried on,
'but I need to check that all we have to do is light the
touchpaper and stand back.' She was gabbling now,
talking nonsense, eager to get away before he realised
how upset she was. Luc's ability to close himself off
was notorious, but it hurt when he raised those same
barricades to her. 'I'll keep in touch,' she promised.
'I'll bring you and your people into a team meeting,
if you like?'

'Of course,' he insisted. 'And let me know the result of the test right away, and what the doctor says. And if you need anything—'

'I'll let you know,' she cut across him as her heart threatened to shatter into tiny pieces.

CHAPTER TWELVE

SHE HAD TO close her mind to Luc and that wasn't easy. Thankfully her forward planning had borne fruit. The Party Planners team was ready to roll. Everything was in place. They could hold the event this very minute without a hitch. The biggest and most glamorous party of the season had taken over everyone's thinking, and now it must take over hers, Stacey determined.

She hadn't even asked where to find him. Luc hadn't asked her—

Her throat dried as she remembered that she had his contact details safely logged in her file, where Luc and everything else to do with him should have remained.

Caressing her stomach, she thought, *Not everything.*

Lucas was a vitally important client, and she and the team had this chance to build on their success in Barcelona. She couldn't allow her personal concerns to get in the way of that. 'Go, team!' she said as their meeting broke up. 'This is going to be the most amazing event yet.'

* * *

He stowed his skis at a local hotel he owned, then had a meeting with his people, who confirmed arrangements for the party were well under way, and there was nothing for him to worry about. *Except Stacey.* His guts were in knots. News of a possible pregnancy had bulldozed every thought from his head. It was a relief to know that the business side of things was going well. He doubted he could sort a problem with the party in his current state of mind.

Leaving the hotel to pace the streets to eat up time until he could reasonably call Stacey for the promised meeting, he spotted her leaving the pharmacy. Jogging across the road, he caught up with her. 'Coffee. Now,' he prescribed, glancing across the road at a café with steamed-up windows.

'Don't we have a meeting?'

She seemed pale to him. 'You need warming up. Business can wait.'

'Isn't the café a bit public for you?' she asked with concern.

'Aren't you exposed out here on your own with a pregnancy test clutched in your hand?' he countered.

'Don't,' she bit out tensely. 'Don't do this to me, Luc.'

'Don't do what?' he asked, uncomprehending.

'Just stop it, okay?'

Her voice was tight, and, though she kept her face turned away from him, he cursed himself for being a fool. Stacey could never handle kindness. Aside from her brother's care it was out of her ken. 'Okay.

I'll back off,' he agreed. 'What you do and when you do it is up to you. All I ask is that you keep me informed. We could be starting a dynasty here.' His last remark was a failed attempt to lighten the mood, and the look she gave him could strip paint. He deserved it and stuck out his chin. 'Go on. Hit me,' he offered. 'You'll feel better if you do.'

'No. That's a man thing, Luc.' And then she smiled faintly. 'Coffee sounds good to me. And then I've got some more work to do,' she hurried to add.

'Of course,' he said, dipping his head in apparent meek submission. 'Whatever you say, *señorita*.'

Her look now said as clearly as if she'd spoken the words out loud: *But it's always whatever you say, Luc.* Swiftly followed by defiant eyes that warned him to get ready for a change of regime. If anything could persuade him she was pregnant, it was that, and not the test she'd bought at the pharmacy. Stacey remembered his mother's care for her children; she would have died for them. And she had.

Luc looked as wound up as she felt, which was why she had agreed to a coffee before their meeting. And so here they were in a cosy café, sipping hot drinks, surrounded by happy people on holiday, and even some of Luc's guests, whom he greeted with enthusiasm, as if he and they shouldn't and didn't have a care in the world. However incongruous it seemed to Stacey with a pregnancy test stuffed securely in the zip-up pocket of her snowsuit, she was the lover of this man, his possibly pregnant lover…

What was she? What was she really? Was she Luc's friend? His lover? His girlfriend?

Or did she merely work for him, and had been his 'bit on the side'?

None of the above, Stacey concluded as Luc shook his head as he stood talking to a group who knew him, causing his thick black hair to fly about his face. This exposed the gold hoop in his ear that glittered a warning to all and sundry—except to Stacey, who was blind to common sense when Luc was in the picture—that this was Lucas Da Silva, consummate lover, ruthless polo player, hard man of business, and a bona fide Spanish grandee who mixed in the most exalted circles, and who it sometimes seemed only resembled Stacey in as much as they both liked a good cup of coffee.

While they'd been stranded in his chalet she'd lost sight of the depth of his complexity. Luc didn't belong to her, he belonged to the world, to this world, to this sophisticated world, where she had never been comfortable. Being brought up on a farm hadn't given her airs and graces, it had given her grit. And now she could be having this man's child. It hardly seemed possible. Until her body throbbed a pleasurable reminder that it was.

'Okay?' he asked, coming to sit down again at their table. 'Excuse me for leaving you. As you could see, duty called.'

As it always would for both of them. What type of foundation was that for a child?

'You look cold,' he said. 'Come on, drink up that coffee. It will warm you.'

If only life were that simple. There was no offer to warm her from Luc, she noticed, but they were in public now. 'It's cold outside,' she commented lightly, looking out of the window.

'Understatement,' Luc agreed in the same disappointingly neutral tone. 'They're saying it might snow again.'

When he'd held her in his arms, she'd been warm enough. It was only when they'd reached the village that a chill had started creeping through her veins. It was the chill of anticipated loss of Luc when they parted, rather than anything she could blame on the weather. Though snow had started falling again, she noted with concern.

'Weather conditions will impact everything,' she observed. 'Where possible, I've accounted for every eventuality.'

'And where it's not possible?' he probed.

'I'm still worried about getting people up the mountain for your torchlit descent and the firework display.'

'Leave that to me.'

'Really?'

'I have an idea.'

'Let me know as soon as you can.'

'I will,' he promised, holding her gaze. 'And you let me know as soon as you can.'

'Of course.' Her heart lifted as she realised Luc hadn't forgotten anything. 'If we can get this right your guests will be talking about this party for the rest of their lives.'

'And you?' he pressed with a keen stare. 'What will you be talking about, Stacey?'

'Happy times.' She pressed her lips flat as her eyes smiled. 'I won't let you down,' she promised.

'Okay?'

'Not sure.' The strangest feeling had just swept over her. It was the same not-alone-in-her-body feeling she'd had before. First stop: a bathroom.

'I'm relying on you to get this right,' Lucas said, draining his cup.

She nodded, half in business mode, half planning to dash off right away to see the doctor at the drop-in clinic. 'I won't let you down. It's going to be the event of the year.' The event of *her life* if she was pregnant.

'What would you like to eat?'

'No time to eat. The bathroom?' she reminded him. 'Coffee's fine.'

'Soup,' he said. 'You must eat something.'

'Okay, soup,' she agreed. 'But this one's on me.'

Luc had relaxed a little over a bowl of soup, and now she was on her way to one of the last briefings with her team before the big event with a pregnancy test stuffed in her pocket.

As they'd parted, he'd said, 'Thank you for bringing me up to speed regarding the party, and now I must speak with my people.'

There'd been no mention of seeing each other again, but she'd taken that for granted, she supposed. Luc would obviously want to know the result of the test.

'Your global empire calling?' she'd teased.

'Well, I'm more concerned about the party right now,' he'd admitted, 'as it's only a couple of days away, but, yes, the global empire is always waiting in the wings. I never know from one day to the next when I'll be called away at a moment's notice.'

A cold wind had brushed her cheek when he'd said that but, keeping her promise to herself that she wouldn't become a clinging vine, she'd simply nodded her head in agreement.

They'd done a lot of reminiscing over lunch, leaving out details like how it felt to make love after wanting and caring and needing for so long. Or how safe she'd felt when Luc had steered her down the mountain. They hadn't mentioned taste, touch, or sensation, but it had been there all the time in their eyes—the glance that had lasted a beat too long, the small shrug of resignation that things couldn't be different between them, because of who they were, and the very different paths they trod. Luc's first memory of Stacey at the farm had been waking up in the morning to discover she'd squirted shaving cream into his hand while he was asleep, so the minute he raked his hair, he was covered in the stuff. 'I remember your roar of fury,' she'd told him with relish.

He'd looked like a great angry bear when he'd stomped out of his room in search of the bathroom with foam all over his face. She'd suspected at the time that no one treated Lucas Da Silva with such scant regard for his position in life, for, though his parents had been impoverished, they'd been aristocrats with a lineage stretching back through the mists of time. 'And the chilli in my ice cream,' he'd reminded her.

'It was strawberry, so I thought you wouldn't notice. Clever, huh?' she'd said with a mischievous look over the rim of her coffee cup.

'Deadly,' he'd agreed, and then they'd laughed together before falling silent again.

Would she never lose this yearning for Lucas? The more she saw of him, the more she liked him. She couldn't help herself.

And what was wrong with that?

Everything, Stacey concluded as she entered the hotel where the team was waiting. She was setting herself up to be hurt.

CHAPTER THIRTEEN

WHAT WAS SHE doing now? What was the result of the test? What was the doctor's view?

These were his thoughts as his jet soared into the sky, leaving the mountains and Stacey behind. An emergency call to return to London had necessitated an immediate change of plan. He'd ring her when he landed. No panic. She'd be busy with last-minute arrangements and he'd see her at the party. If anyone could cope, it was Stacey. He'd tried to call her several times, but her phone was always engaged. She occupied his thoughts in ways that left no room for anything else—not for business, for the all-important annual party to thank his best customers and staff, nor even his siblings and the fellow members of the Da Silva polo team.

What could be more important to him than the fact that he and Stacey might be expecting a child?

On that thought, he called her again.

Her phone rang out.

She would be busy, he reassured himself. He'd called in at the hotel where mammoth structures for his party were already being created, but no one had been able to find her. He'd guessed she was at the drop-in clinic. Her plans to delight and amaze his guests had exceeded even his jaundiced expectations, but now, instead of seeing towering structures mimicking an ice kingdom, or animatronic dragons breathing fire on demand over a banqueting hall of unsurpassed splendour, his mind was full of Stacey, and how beautiful she'd looked when they'd skied down the mountain. Cheeks flushed, eyes bright with excitement, snowflakes frosting soft auburn tendrils framing her face, she'd appeared lovelier to him than he'd ever seen her.

If he had a different life and could shake the guilt that haunted him, and Stacey weren't welded to her career, they might be planning a very different future. As it was, they must both be tense as they waited for the result of the pregnancy test, and he only wished he could be there to reassure her. But that was his life. That was his solitary life, and she was better out of it.

He called her again.

No reply.

So it was true. She wasn't going crazy, Stacey reflected as she left the walk-in clinic with a sheaf of leaflets advising on pregnancy and what to expect. Just as she'd suspected, the feeling inside her was a miraculous spark of new life. She was jubilant and terrified, as well as full of determination and purpose, all at once. Jubilant because it was a miracle she embraced with all her heart, and terrified because she didn't exactly have a pattern to follow, or a guidebook to help her, let alone a mother to advise and promise that it didn't have to be like the childhood Stacey remembered, full of mental anguish and regret. It could be a happy time. It *would* be a happy time, she determined as she pulled out her phone to call Lucas. Their child would be happy. She'd give her life to that cause.

No way!

Her phone was flat!

She'd been rather too busy over the past twenty-four hours to think about charging her phone. Exhaling noisily with frustration, she determined to call him as soon as she arrived at the hotel.

But as she crunched across the snow-covered pavement, the panic to call him subsided. Part of her wanted to tell him right away, while another part wanted to keep the news in a tight little kernel in her chest just a little while longer. Sharing things at home in the past had always got her shot down in flames. She knew Luc was a very different man from her father, but the past was a powerful enemy.

And she was stronger. Mothers had to be the strongest of all.

Once she had charged up her phone, she resolved to call him.

'He's been called away?' she repeated, bewildered, once she got through.

Luc's phone was on call divert and she was speaking to one of his PAs. The woman was to the point, rather than sympathetic. 'I'm afraid I can't give you any more information, but I will pass on the message that you called.'

'Thank y—'

The line was already dead.

You've never had any hand-holding, so why do you need it now?

Correct. She'd got this.

Those were Stacey's exact thoughts two days later as she stared into the mirror before heading off to the Da Silva party, where, regardless of how she felt inside, she couldn't wait to showcase the talents of her team. The thought of seeing Luc again was a constant thrum of excitement that she was fully aware would play in the background of everything she did that night. She'd deal with that too.

This particular event was difficult to dress for, as there were so many elements to the night. First there would be a champagne reception, followed by a traditional banquet with dancing and an auction afterwards at the hotel in the village. Then a trip up the mountain to the balcony of Luc's chalet, which was the ideal vantage point for a firework display, and then later the famous torchlit procession of the most expert skiers in the area, who would descend a mountain floodlit by snow tractors. Thermals beneath a ball gown were a sensible precaution to cater for everything the weather could throw at her, and she had snow boots at the ready.

Luc had arranged an ingenious mode of transport

to get guests up the mountain after the main party in the hotel. They made a great team, she mused as she checked her make-up in the mirror. Or might have done, if he'd troubled to speak to her. Everything was being conducted through their teams, so Luc had obviously made his decision regarding any possible future for them. If he had got in touch she could have told him the happy truth. Perhaps it was as well they kept things this way, though she couldn't deny his behaviour surprised her. Luc wasn't the type to turn his back on anything, but he had, and of all things, on the possibility of becoming a father. She didn't know whether to pity him for being more damaged than she'd thought, or whether she should regard herself as just another of his discards. Either way, it hurt. Once this party wrapped they wouldn't be part of each other's lives. Their amazing fling was over. There was no way anything could happen between them in the real world, their paths were too different, as were their dreams.

So...?

Swinging a lanyard around her neck, she blinked back tears. *So, go, team! Go, Stacey!* Make this the best party ever, adding another brick in the foundations you're building for your child.

His first sight of Stacey sucked the air from his lungs. The gown she'd chosen to wear was a deep shade of blue that contrasted beautifully with her rich auburn hair and Celtic colouring. She was wearing her hair up tonight, displaying those incredible cheekbones and her lush, generous mouth. She was easily the most attractive woman at the party, and it took an effort to drag his gaze away to concentrate on his guests.

This was quite literally an evening for the great and good. Some of the guests were undeniably pompous, and some were snobs he could have done without, but the various charities he supported needed their money. There were those who were fabulously rich and correspondingly stupid, and he could never understand how they held onto their wealth. He had also invited members of his staff from across the world, pearls beyond price without whom nothing would get done, as well as representatives from each of the charities.

And then there was Stacey.

His gaze kept stealing back to her, and each time he looked her way she was being equally gracious to everyone. Whether she was greeting a member of the aristocracy, one of the many ambassadors he'd invited, a group of cleaners from his London office, or a head of government, she behaved with the same gentle charm. His only regret was that her brother couldn't be here tonight to see her as he was seeing her, but Niahl was with the team playing polo. He hadn't told Niahl how far his relationship with his sister had progressed, but they knew each other too well for Niahl not to notice how many times Stacey had cropped up in conversation. 'Take care of her,' Niahl had said. 'That's all I ask. Above anyone I know my sister deserves to be happy.' A spear of regret hit him at the thought that he had pretty much allowed this unique woman to slip through his fingers without even putting up a fight. He'd allowed business to take precedence over Stacey, and even the possibility of a child.

One day he would have to confront his feelings, and could only pray that by the time he got around to doing so, it wouldn't be too late.

He watched her deal with more difficult guests, and felt anger on her behalf that she turned herself inside out for everyone, but who cared for Stacey? Who massaged her shoulders after an evening like this when she was exhausted? Who would kiss the nape of her neck, fix her a drink and bank up the fire to keep her warm?

'Señor Da Silva!'

He wheeled around to face an elderly Spanish duke.

'What a pleasure! What a party! You have quite a find in Señorita Winner. I'd hold onto her if I were you.'

'Don Alejandro,' he said, smiling warmly as he gripped his compatriot's hand. 'So delighted you could make it.'

'Not half as delighted as I am, Lucas. Take my advice for once and hold onto her.'

He didn't need advice to do that, Lucas reflected as his elegant friend went to join his companions at their table. But in all probability he'd already blown it.

He'd greeted all the guests, and now there was just one more thing to do.

He stood in Stacey's way as she patrolled the ball-room. 'Are you avoiding me?'

Seeing him, she tensed, but her eyes darkened as she looked up at him to ask coolly, 'Should I?'

'You are the most infuriating woman,' he said as he backed her into the shadows.

'Lucas, I'm busy.'

'Too busy to talk to your most important client?' But there was a lot more than business in his eyes. She knew what he wanted to know.

'You're here to talk business,' she said. 'Of course, I'm not too busy to speak to you, Señor Da Silva.'

'Luc, surely?'

'What can I do for you, Señor Da Silva?'

She was a cool one, but there was a flicker of sadness in her eyes.

'I want to congratulate you on a fabulous evening, of course.'

'It isn't over yet.'

He raised a brow and had the satisfaction of seeing her blush.

'Is there something I can get for you?'

'We'll talk about that later. I notice you plan to hold an auction after the banquet, and there are some truly spectacular prizes.'

'You have very generous friends.'

'And you can be very persuasive.'

She said nothing, refusing as always to take any praise. The tension between them was extraordinary.

'A silent auction,' he observed.

'Yes. It's less intrusive, and goes on longer—all

night,' she explained. 'The prizes remain on view, either in here on tables at the far end of the ballroom, or in a photograph. To place a bid on a certain lot, all your guests have to do is place their offer in a sealed envelope. Competition is fierce, as no one has any idea what anyone else has bid.'

'Smart woman.'

'Did you think I was stupid?'

'No,' he said in the same easy, conversational tone she had used. 'I admire you.'

'It's my job,' she dismissed with a shrug. 'I promised to do my best for you, and I will. There's no chance to show off, but no one wants to miss out.' Her eyes bored into his. 'So the charities benefit far more from these secret bids than they would from a noisy auction.'

'Excellent.' He dipped his head in approval while every fibre of his body demanded that he claim her now. 'I approve. Well, you'd better get on.'

'Yes, sir.'

'Luc,' he reminded her through gritted teeth. 'We'll see each other at the end of the evening.'

Stacey's eyes flashed open. *Oh, will we?* she thought.

Her heart twisted into knots of confusion as Luc walked away. She hated that he could shake her professional persona to this extent, yet she longed for a glance that said he cared. She expected too much. Always had. Her father had told her that frequently, and he was right. She was needy inside and had to shrug it off and don her armour.

It wasn't easy to ignore Luc, and as she worked the room she watched him. With his easy stride and magnificent physique—a body she could undress in her mind at a moment's notice—he was outrageously hot, a fact she could see being logged by every sentient being in the room. It reminded her of when she'd been the wallflower on the bench and admirers had mobbed him. Would she see him after the party? She could be cynical all she liked, but her heart leapt at the thought.

Stacey's silent auction proved to be a brilliant idea, and was an incredible success. He wanted to congratulate her, but, as usual, she was impossible to find. Eventually, she almost crashed into him on her way to find an extra drum to hold all the bids. 'Kudos to you,' he called out as she rushed past. With every base covered at this, his most important event of the year, she had exceeded his expectations by a considerable amount.

There were so many bids to count he thought they'd never be finished, but when the final total was announced, the money raised for the various charities was a record amount. He'd tried celebrities and royalty before, but nothing had worked like this. Stacey should share the spotlight with him, he determined as he mounted the stage. He called for her but there was no answer from the crowd. Shrugging this off with a smile to reassure his audience, he told them she was probably hard at work on his next event and raised a laugh. Turning to his aide, he added in a very different tone, 'Find her.'

He strode from the stage to tumultuous applause that should have been Stacey's. 'On second thoughts,' he said, catching his aide's elbow before the man could leave, 'I'll find her.'

Stacey was sitting alone in the office her team was using as a temporary base in the hotel. She could hear cheers in the distance, and guessed the amount of money raised by the auction had just been announced, but this was one of the few opportunities she would have during the night to be alone, and she had just realised that she couldn't 'suck it up' as she'd thought, as Lucas remained resolutely centred in her mind. Anything he did or said affected her. However pathetic that was, it was a fact she had to deal with. There was no possibility of conveniently ejecting him from her mind. At the same time, she was alert for the end of this part of the evening. Transport was already waiting outside for the guests. She'd scheduled everyone's departure, so there was no need to show her face yet. The team had done its work, begging for prizes, and then organising and displaying them to best advantage, and she was more than happy to leave the glory to them and to Lucas. Raising money for good causes was something he did extremely well, and the auction was always a high point for Stacey. Tonight had seen a phenomenal result, mainly due to the fact that Lucas had an incredible array of wealthy friends. She'd noticed the sideways glances between the rich and famous as they'd attempted to outbid each other. In a silent auction no one knew what anyone else was bidding, so the temptation was always to add a little more, which was all to the good for the charities.

Leaning back in the chair, she closed her eyes and sighed with relief. Chalking up another success should have her buzzing with excitement. It would secure the immediate future of the company, and she was optimistic about requests for quotations flooding in once the press spread the word of another stunning Party Planners event. But it also heralded the end of working with Lucas.

A child should bring them together, if only for the occasional meeting, but would he want that? His attitude so far had been distant in the extreme, and she didn't want him dropping in and out of their lives. Their baby needed both its parents—not living together, necessarily, but both equally invested in its current and future well-being. So much for his talk of a dynasty, she reflected with a small sad laugh. If he took this much interest in his line going forward, it would die out.

She started with surprise as the door burst open and Luc walked in. 'There you are,' he exclaimed as if she'd been hiding. 'Come with me. I want to introduce you on stage so you can take credit for your success.'

It took her a moment to rejig her brain back into work mode. Luc was like a tornado who swept in and then out again with equal force. Taking a deep breath, she asked the only question that mattered where business was concerned. 'Has the team been on stage?'

'Of course,' he said impatiently. 'But you weren't there.'

You make it so inviting, she mused tensely.

'You're part of the team, aren't you?' he demanded.

'Yes, but—'

'No buts,' he said. 'This is your night. And if you won't take the praise for yourself, then at least take it for the team, and for the hotel staff that has supported them.'

Put like that she had no option.

CHAPTER FOURTEEN

THE CROWD IN the ballroom listened attentively as Stacey thanked them for their generous contributions. Then she invited key members of staff up on stage. 'Nothing would happen without these people,' she explained to a barrage of cheers and stamping feet. 'And now, if you would like to join us in the hotel lobby, your transport awaits! And please, dress up warmly. I'll meet you outside, where my team will show you where to go.'

She left the stage as people rushed to grab their coats and boots from the cloakroom. Luc was waiting at the foot of the steps. 'Thank you,' he said politely. 'I know this is your job and what you're paid for, but you've excelled yourself tonight, and I couldn't be more pleased.'

'Thank you,' she said with a tight smile, before hurrying away to join the growing crowd in the hotel lobby.

Was that it? Thank you? Was that all he had to say?

She felt sick inside.

Trying not to think too hard, she smilingly arranged the excited guests into travelling groups. If she dwelled on Luc's manner, she'd break down. She knew it was time to grow up—this was work—but if only he could be a little less distant, and maybe ask some intelligent questions about the baby. His disregard hurt so much, she had to believe there was a reason for it. He couldn't have changed so much, become so cold. She knew he had a problem with feelings, but taking it to these lengths? There had to be something wrong.

Get over it. It was probably all for the good, she decided as she started to muster guests into travelling groups. She would never belong in this sophisticated world. If they could return to the easy relationship they'd shared on the farm when they weren't fighting, chatting easily about horses, maybe there'd be a chance for them. She huffed a humourless laugh as she moved on to the next group of guests.

Operation Up the Mountain was a welcome distraction. Stacey's passion remained unchanged. Seeing people enjoy themselves at the events she organised was everything to her, and she never allowed personal feelings to get in the way. It was crucial that guests remained unaware of the mechanics behind an event, and it never felt like work to Stacey. But to be on the receiving end of this carousel of parties and lunches, banquets and fashion shows, rather than organising them? She couldn't do it. She had to get her hands dirty. She had to be real. False eyelashes wouldn't last five minutes in the country in a rainstorm, and, though she loved the city and all the glamorous occasions she helped to arrange, her long-term goal was to live on a small farm surrounded by ponies, where the only event she ever went to was the local county show.

The transport Luc had arranged was inspired. Nothing could stop the big snowploughs trundling up the mountain on their tank treads. Headlights blazing, music blaring, the party continued as they travelled up the slope. Stacey found herself seated next to Lucas, but this was business so she kept her distance and he kept his. The only comments they made were directed at their guests to make sure they were seated comfortably and well wrapped up in rugs.

When they arrived at Luc's impressive chalet, she'd made sure that champagne, mulled wine and soft drinks were waiting for his guests.

'You've thought of everything,' he commented as he helped her to climb down. 'And you look amazing.'

She blinked. Not that Luc's touch on her arm wasn't as electrifying as ever, or his face as wonderfully familiar, nor were the expressive eyes holding her own bemused stare any less darkly commanding and beautiful, but…compliments? Really? Was that the best way to start when they had so much more to say to each other?

So what would you say? She shrugged inwardly. He'd made a start. She should too. 'You don't look bad yourself. We'll talk later. Yes?'

Angling a strong chin already liberally shaded with stubble, Luc gave her a measured look. 'I think I can make time for you.'

'Make sure you do.' And with that she was off about her duties.

He tracked her down in an empty kitchen minutes before the fireworks and the torchlit descent were due to start. 'I sent Maria out to enjoy the show,' she explained in a neutral tone, swiping a cloth across the granite worktops without pausing to look up.

'Well?' he prompted, suffocated by tension he could cut with a knife. 'Do you have some news for me?'

She stilled and slowly raised her head. 'Are you saying you don't know?'

Of course he knew. He made it his business to know everything concerning him. His security team hadn't been hired for their pretty faces. But he wanted Stacey to tell him. Whether she could open up enough to do so remained to be seen. 'Just tell me.'

'Congratulations,' she said in the same emotion-free tone. 'You're going to be a daddy.'

He ground his jaw so hard he could have cracked some teeth. The way she'd told him, and, worse, the way this most marvellous news was overshadowed by concerns from his past, made him madder than hell, and saddened him equally.

'Don't you have anything to say?' she pressed.

'Congratulations,' he echoed with a brief, accepting smile.

'Wow. Your enthusiasm overwhelms me.'

'Not now,' he warned as Maria bustled back into the kitchen.

'When, then?' Stacey mouthed across the counter.

'When everyone else has left and we're alone.'

With a shrug she seemed to accept this, and they split, each attending to their duties, which left them both, he suspected, with a grinding impatience that wouldn't leave them until they'd talked.

The most spectacular firework display Stacey had ever seen was accompanied by classical music. The combination of fire in the sky and the passionate strains of a full orchestra turned a spectacular event into a spellbinding affair. She couldn't resist watching for a while, though tensed when Luc joined her. She didn't need to turn around to know he was there.

'Enjoying it?' he asked.

'It's amazing,' she confirmed. 'But shouldn't you be spending time with your guests?'

'Shouldn't you?' he countered softly.

'Of course, *señor*—'

'For goodness' sake, don't call me that. And no. Stay with me,' he commanded, catching hold of her arm when she started to move away. 'I want to watch the display with *you*. My guests won't care with all this going on.'

'I guess not,' Stacey agreed as a starburst of light exploded high in the night sky over their heads. Luc didn't speak as he came to stand close behind her. He made no attempt to touch her, but that didn't stop all the tiny hairs on the back of her neck standing to attention. She could almost imagine his heat warming her, and she found herself wanting to forget their differences and start again. More than anything she wanted them both to throw off the shackles of the past and express themselves freely to the extent that Luc took her in his arms and kissed her in front of everyone, and she kissed him back. But that was never going to happen when a muted 'Congratulations' was the best he could manage at the news of their child.

He wanted to drag her into his arms and kiss the breath from her lungs, but not with so many interested eyes on them. It hadn't been easy for Stacey to build a new life, and the last thing he wanted was to cast the shadow of his so-called celebrity over her, bringing her to the world's interest. Her childhood and early teens had largely been composed of fantasies, Niahl had told him, and that was to block out the fact that she felt invisible at home. Stacey's only fault was being a reminder of her mother. She'd tried hard to shake that off, but in doing so had ended up feeling disloyal to her mother's memory. She couldn't win. From the youngest age she hadn't been able to do right in her father's eyes, and that had stripped her confidence bare. She had worked hard when she left home to build up her self-belief, and he could so easily destroy it with a few misjudged words. Everything he said to Stacey had to be weighed carefully, and, unfortunately, like her, he was a man with a tendency to spit things out.

Deciding there was only one way around the problem, he knew that it wasn't enough to rejoice in the fact that they were having a baby, and that Stacey would always know he was holding something back. The only answer was to unlock the darkest secret from his past and confront it, but that would have to wait, as the torchlit descent in which he was taking part was about to begin.

'I'm sorry… I have to go,' he explained. 'My job is to ride shotgun and make sure no one falls or gets left behind.'

'I understand,' she said with a quick smile before glancing back at the chalet. 'And I need to make sure that everyone's glass is full to toast the parade as you start off.'

'You'll be okay if I leave you here?'

She shot him a look and smiled. 'I'll be okay,' she confirmed, but her gaze didn't linger on his face as it once had, and he knew that if he lost her trust it would be gone for ever. Stacey was a survivor who knew when to cut a hopeless cause loose. He ground his jaw at the thought that he was in real danger of falling into that category, and right now there was nothing he could do about it. The ski instructors and other advanced skiers were waiting for him on the slope. He was one of the stewards, and the torchlit descent couldn't begin until he was on his skis, ready to go with them. 'Don't get cold,' he warned Stacey.

She laughed. 'Don't worry. I won't. I'll be far too busy for that.'

* * *

After making sure all the guests had a drink, and a blanket if they needed one, Stacey chose a good vantage point. She had selected the music to accompany the skiers' decent in a sentimental moment, asking the guitarist from Barcelona, where she had so memorably danced with Luc, if he would agree to play live with a full orchestra, and he had agreed. Everyone around her commented on the passion and beauty with which he played, and as the other instruments swelled in a crescendo behind him her eyes filled with tears at the thought that special moments like these could never be recaptured.

But they would live on in the memory. Cling on to that...

She must not cry. This wasn't the time or the place, so she bit down hard on her bottom lip. Luc's guests relied on her to entertain them and their evening wasn't over yet. Personal feelings were unimportant. She'd be better off without them, and must certainly never show them. Maybe she had revealed too much to Lucas, because what had he shared with her? He kept more hidden than he revealed.

Her thoughts were abruptly cut short when everything was plunged into darkness, signalling the start of the descent. The murmur of anticipation around her died. Nothing was visible beyond the ghostly white peaks. Then the lights of the same snowploughs that had brought the guests up the mountain blazed into life and it was possible to see the skiers assembling with their torches like tiny dots of light. She wished Luc safe with all her heart. It reassured her to know that the chief mountain guide always led the procession, as no one knew the ever-changing nature of the trail better than he. Skiing at night at speed always held some risk, and there had been fallers. Not this year, she prayed fervently as she fixed her gaze on the top of the slope.

The long snake of light with its accompanying music was an unforgettable sight and Stacey was as spellbound as the rest. As if one party wasn't enough, there would be another in the village square to welcome everyone safely home. Transport was waiting for Luc's guests, and as she moved amongst them it was wonderful to feel their upbeat mood. The feedback so far suggested this was the most successful event Party Planners had ever arranged. It was just a shame the lights went out at the end of it, Stacey reflected, pressing her lips flat with regret.

The snowplough was approaching the village, where she could see that every shop and restaurant was ablaze with light. There were bunting and bands in the square and so many food kiosks they were banked up side by side. This was the first real fun people had been able to enjoy since the village had been snowbound, and everyone was determined to make the most of it. And it didn't take long, once they had been taken down, to learn that the roads were clear, and everything was on the move again.

She glanced around, but couldn't see Lucas. Quartering the square in the hope of finding him proved useless; there was no sign of him. None of the guests had seen their host and the torchlit descent had ended some time ago. So where was he?

'Some people peel away and ski home before they reach the village,' a ski guide still pumped with success and effort told her. 'Maybe Lucas is one of these. He's very popular...'

As the guys around him laughed Stacey walked away, red-faced, but she couldn't give up. Maybe Lucas had gone home with another woman, but that was his business. She just wanted to know he was safe. And it didn't seem likely that he'd desert his guests. At last, she found someone who'd seen him.

'He stopped on the slopes to help a young woman who was trailing behind, and then she fell,' the elderly man informed her.

'Not badly hurt, I hope?' she exclaimed.

'The clinic's just over there,' he said, pointing it out. 'You could go and ask.'

'Thank you. I will.' She had to know for sure what was happening. If Lucas didn't show his face, she'd have to explain to his guests why their host had deserted them. Summoning reinforcements from the team on the radio to look after the guests milling about the square, she crossed the road to the clinic. Each small community in the mountains had a medical facility and a doctor on standby. She'd discovered this while she'd been researching the area for information to pass on to the guests.

The receptionist at the clinic explained that Lucas had stopped to help a young woman, but the young woman had turned out to be only thirteen years old, and skiing on the mountain without the consent of her parents. 'It isn't the first time and it won't be the last,' the smiling receptionist told Stacey. 'The mountain is like a magnet to local teenagers, and the annual parade is the biggest draw of all.'

'Can I help you?'

Breath shot from her lungs. '*Lucas!* Thank goodness you're safe!'

Regardless of anything that had gone before, she was just so relieved to see him.

Still dressed in dark ski wear, he looked exactly like the type of big, swarthy hero any young woman would dream of sweeping her off her feet on the slope. It was lucky she was Lucas-proof, Stacey reflected as he shot her a brooding look.

'Why are you here?' he demanded coolly.

'To find you, of course.'

'Shouldn't you be with my guests?'

'Shouldn't you?' She stared up at him, unblinking, while her heart shouted hallelujah to see him unharmed.

'Are you here to remind me of my manners?'

'If you need a nudge…?'

A glint of humour in his eyes greeted this remark.

'How is the girl you rescued?'

'A painful pulled ligament. Thankfully, nothing more.'

'And you're okay?' She searched his eyes.

'Obviously.'

Why didn't she believe him? Because the wounds

Luc carried weren't visible, Stacey concluded as he glanced at the exit.

'I'm going to say goodnight to my guests,' he explained, 'and then I'm going to take you home. I've checked the girl's parents are on their way, so there's nothing more for me to do here except thank the staff and hold the door for you.'

'I can stay in the hotel in the village,' she protested. 'People are leaving now the roads are clear.'

'The gondolas are running too,' Luc commented as they left the building, ignoring her last comment, 'so no excuses. You're coming with me.'

They needed to talk, she reasoned, so why not? Just because Luc was unconventional and unpredictable didn't mean they couldn't communicate successfully. Demanding clients were her stock in trade. How much harder could it be to discuss the future of their child with Luc?

After an extensive round of farewells, Stacey was able to wrap up the night with her team, and Luc led the way up the steps of the gondola station. 'Come on,' he encouraged. 'We can have a car to ourselves.'

Grabbing her hand, he pulled her into an empty car just as the doors were closing.

CHAPTER FIFTEEN

'Luc—' As THE gondola started off she was thrown against him. Pressing her hands against his chest, she reminded him that they hadn't even talked about the baby.

'You're well,' he said, 'and that's all that matters.'

And then he closed off.

'And those guests you couldn't find to say good-night to?' she pressed, wanting some reaction from him.

'I'll see them at the airport tomorrow. Tonight is for you.'

For sex, she assumed. Not that she didn't crave Luc's body, but she wanted more from him. She had other concerns on her mind, notably an unborn child.

'You're taking a lot for granted,' she observed, steadying herself on the hand rail.

'Yes,' he agreed. 'I want to spend the night with you.'

Her pulse went crazy, but she had to accept that nothing had changed. How many times had they been

together without Luc opening up? And she had to
know the father of her child. They could be so close
in so many ways, and complete strangers in others.
He shut her out when she needed to be sure that Luc
bore no resemblance to her own father. She couldn't
bear that. She wouldn't bear it, and neither would her
child. No infant should be shunned, and if Luc was
incapable of expressing his feelings, then perhaps
she should keep him at a distance. What was it in
his past that had made him so insular? She was bad
enough, but he was gold standard when it came to
hiding his feelings. If she couldn't find out tonight,
what chance did she have?

'We will talk?' she pressed.

'Of course we will,' he promised.

'When?'

'Soon.'

'Should I be satisfied with that?'

He raised a brow and smiled down, forcing her to
realise that she had underestimated his devastating
appeal. Luc only had to look at her a certain way for
her scruples to vanish. 'No, we can't,' she protested
as he dragged her close.

'Where does it say that in the rule book?' he murmured. 'You carry around a very heavy rule book,
Señorita Winner, but it's not one I care to read.'

'Seriously, Lucas…'

'I intend to be very serious indeed, as I'm dealing
with an emergency situation.'

*One more night with the man she loved. What
could be wrong with that?*

Everything, Stacey's cautious inner voice suggested. *You'll miss him even more when he's gone.*

So be it, she concluded as Luc drove his mouth down on hers.

Arranging her to his liking, with her legs around his waist, he supported her with his big hands wrapped around her buttocks.

'Are you sure I'm not too heavy?'

'What do you think?' he said, slowly sinking to the hilt.

She was thinking that she would never get used to this…to Luc wanting her, and to the feeling of completeness that gave her—or to the size of him. 'What do I think?' she asked on a gasp. 'Take me gently.'

'Gently?' he queried as he drew back to plunge again.

'The baby,' she reminded him.

'I can do gentle,' he murmured, proving this in the most effective way. 'Though you should know that babies are quite resilient.'

With a smile she shook her head. 'You did your research on that too?'

'Let's find out,' Luc suggested, and from that moment on he had her exclaiming rhythmically as she urged him on to take her repeatedly on the journey to the top station. It was long enough for several mind-shattering bouts of pleasure, and by the time they'd straightened their clothes and stepped out of the small cabin, she was committed to spending the rest of the night with Luc. Anything else would not only be wrong, it would be inconceivable. She wanted him too much to resist him. Pregnancy had made her mad for sex, and Luc was only too willing to help her with that.

They fell on each other the moment they entered his chalet. The inside of the front door proved a useful surface as he took her again, and while she was still whimpering in the aftershock of pleasure, he carried her over to the sofa in the living room and pressed her down. 'Again!' she demanded fiercely as he moved between her legs.

Luc gave her everything she needed and more, and it was only when she quietened that she thought to ask if they were alone.

'If we weren't to begin with, I imagine you've frightened everyone away by now with your screams.'

Balling her hands into fists, she pummelled him weakly. 'That's not funny, Lucas.'

'Oh, but it is,' he argued as he rolled her on top of him. 'I'm going to strip you, and make love to you again, and you can scream as loudly as you like.'

They moved from sofa to rug in front of a glowing fire where they made love until she fell back, exhausted. 'I'll never forget this trip...or you...us...' she whispered as Luc soothed her down.

'That sounds like goodbye,' he commented, frowning as he pulled back his head to stare into her eyes with concern.

'Not yet, but soon,' she whispered. It was inevitable.

'Not yet,' Luc agreed, brushing smiling kisses

against her mouth, 'because first I'm going to take you to bed.'

'To sleep in each other's arms,' she murmured contentedly as he sprang up and lifted her.

'To sleep in each other's arms,' Luc confirmed.

He watched her sleep. This was fast becoming one of his favourite occupations, he had discovered. Was this caring warmth inside him a sign he was capable of feeling something and could master the guilt?

Was this love?

He huffed a cynical smile. He'd always liked Stacey. A lot. As a teenager she'd driven him crazy, and now he admired her like no one else. But love? Love was dangerous.

She's the mother of my child.

The warmth inside him grew at the thought. There was no one he'd rather choose for that role than Stacey. Brimful with character, integrity, intelligence and determination, she would make a wonderful mother.

On her own again?

If anyone was equal to that task, it was Stacey.

Could I really stand back and let her do that after everything I saw when she was younger? This woman who's been starved of affection will be abandoned again?

Not abandoned. He'd always care for Stacey and their child. She didn't need the additional burden of his guilt to carry around, so this was for the best.

She looked so peaceful he didn't want to wake her.

Exhausted from working tirelessly on behalf of his
guests and from making love for most of the night,
she'd earned her rest. He'd speak to her later about
future arrangements when everyone else had gone.

Slipping out of bed to take a shower, he shrugged
off the memories crowding his mind of warmth and
peace and happiness. They belonged to someone who
deserved them…deserved Stacey. She could safely
sleep on. The first departure for his guests wasn't
due until noon, by which time she'd have a chance to
don her professional face and head out with her usual
sense of purpose to smooth everyone's passage home.

Her work rate pricked his conscience. He wanted
to wake her and make love to her again, but instead
he was heading out to make sure there were no
hitches for her to face. Her charges were his guests
and ultimately his responsibility. She'd done enough
and more besides. He'd catch her later at the airport
with a token of his appreciation to thank her for all
she'd done.

She'd overslept. When did that ever happen? Never.
And she was alone. Luc had gone. Of course he had.
He had work to do.

Didn't she, also?

Everyone remembered the start of an event, and
the event itself, if the planner had got things right,
but what stayed with them was the end, when they
must feel valued enough to hope they might be invited to another similar event.

Leaping out of bed, she snatched up her clothes

and ran to the bathroom. A quick shower later and a scramble to put those same clothes on again, she headed out with a beanie tugged low over her still-damp hair. Glancing out of the window, she saw with relief that the gondolas were running as smoothly as if they'd never stopped.

She was alone in the chalet, no sign of Luc or Maria. She'd grab some breakfast in the village, then head straight for the hotel to make sure the departing guests had everything they needed.

The sky was blue and the skiing was good. As the small cabin swung high above the slopes she searched for him amongst the skiers. There was no sign of him. She longed to see him. They had to talk about the baby before she left for home. Surely he'd open up about that? He must. Whatever was holding him back, he had to put it behind him for the sake of their child. He couldn't be like her father.

She chose the same café where they had eaten before. There were booths where she could be private. She would eat first, settle her mind, and then set out to complete the business side of things. Breezy wait staff brought milky coffee and French toast. She suddenly realised she was ravenous and ordered more. Glancing at her watch, she confirmed that she could afford another few minutes, and her stomach insisted on it.

Her heart jolted when she noticed Luc at the counter, speaking on his phone. He was frowning, but not too preoccupied to thank the staff behind the counter as they loaded his tray. She put her head down as he approached the line of booths where she was sitting. Phone tucked into his shoulder as he walked along, he was holding an intense conversation. She was no eavesdropper, but this was Luc. Whatever he had on his mind, she wanted to help. He looked so serious. What was it? What could it be?

He sat down in the adjoining booth. The seat backs were so high he hadn't seen her.

This wasn't right. She should make herself known.

Why? She wasn't doing any harm.

He was talking to Niahl!

They'd always been a tight unit, she reasoned, and she should have known it was only a matter of time before the bond between them closed her out, relegating her yet again to the tag-along benches; the kid sister to be endured and humoured. She might be older, but she was obviously no wiser, given that the hurt she felt now was so ridiculously intense. Luc was telling her brother they were close and Niahl was ranting. She could hear him…almost as clearly as she could hear Luc's placating reply. 'You're right. I overstepped. It was a huge error of judgement.'

She didn't need to hear more. Throwing some money down on the table, she rushed out. Luc was still talking on the phone as she ran past the window. He hadn't even noticed a woman in distress fleeing the café. That had to be a first for him. The knight in shining armour had clay feet after all.

'You're right, Niahl, and maybe I should have told you sooner, but I wasn't even sure of it myself.'

'Then why were you sleeping with my sister?'

'Stacey isn't like the others. This isn't a fling, Niahl. I love the woman she's become, and I think she loves me.'

'Has she told you this?' Niahl barked suspiciously.

'She doesn't need to.'

'Have you told Stacey that you love her?'

'I'll make it my mission to love and protect her for ever—'

'Have. You. Told. Her?' Niahl roared. 'For God's sake, and yours, don't you think you should?' A colourful curse followed this observation. 'The two of you are hopeless!'

'I love your sister and I'm going to marry her.'

'Maybe you should tell her that too?' Niahl suggested. 'Arrangements take time.'

'You can put your shotgun away. We're going to get married.'

'You hope!' Niahl exploded. 'If you're not too late!'

'I have to tell her something else first.'

There was a long silence, and then Niahl said quietly, 'Yes, you do.'

By sheer force of will, she ground her gears into work mode as she entered the hotel, where she now discovered that everyone was either sleeping, or just not picking up their phone. It had been one hell of a party. Requesting a discreet wake-up call to be delivered to those guests she knew should be leaving for the airport in time for early flights, she now needed something else to do…something to take her mind off what she'd overheard.

Luc had overstepped…

She was a huge error of judgement.

At least she knew where she stood.

Actually, why should he get away with that? Now she was angry. She tried his phone. No answer. With no intention of leaving a message, she headed for the hotel café. She got as far as the entrance when a group of guests saw her, and called her over to their table.

'You'll join us? It's the least we can do. We've had an amazing time, thanks to you.'

'It was a team effort,' she said, embarrassed by the praise.

'Sometimes it's enough to say thank you,' an older woman cautioned with a smile. 'Enjoy it when you're appreciated. You deserve it. You worked hard.'

Was the past responsible for the way she brushed off praise now? Maybe that was because she couldn't quite believe her life had turned around to the extent it had. Did that make her as guilty of hiding her feelings as Luc? Were they both to blame for this situation? She would have to speak to him at some point about their child, but not here, not now, while she was still stinging from what she'd overheard. Niahl used to warn her that she would never hear anything good about herself if she listened in—which she'd used to do when he and Luc were in a huddle discussing their latest adventure. Boy, was he right!

'I agree with my wife.'

Stacey refocused on the kindly face of a man who had spent more money at the charity auction than most people saw in their lifetime. 'I watched you last night and you never stopped. You deserve all the praise you can get. I'm going to tell that man of yours he's found a diamond and should hold onto you.'

'What—? I don't—'

'Understand when a man's madly in love with you?' his wife chipped in. 'Perhaps everyone sees it but you,' she suggested. 'It's obvious to anyone with half an oil field that Lucas Da Silva adores you.'

Stacey gave a fragile laugh. She didn't want to disillusion the couple. Her first and only task was to make sure they got safely on their way. And then the couple made a suggestion that at first she refused and then accepted. 'Thank you. I'd love to,' she said.

Somehow he'd missed her at the hotel, so he gunned the Lamborghini down the highway to the airport. He'd thought a lot about Stacey since speaking to Niahl. *When didn't he think a lot about her?* The thought of losing her was inconceivable, yet Niahl had made it seem a real possibility. It was time to face his demons and explain why he always held part of himself in reserve, and how that had stopped him expressing his feelings. If he got this right they had a lifetime ahead of them. If he failed…

He wouldn't fail.

That was inconceivable.

* * *

'She's gone?' For the first time in his life, he was dumbfounded.

'Yes,' his aide explained, unaware of the turmoil raging inside him. 'Your Texan guest offered Señorita Winner and her team a ride back in his jet. He said it was the least he could do to thank her for giving him and his wife such a wonderful evening.'

She would never have gone without her team. Stacey would never take credit for herself, or fail to share any bonus she might receive. He'd seen her own personal donation to the charity. Sealed bids, maybe, but her handwriting was unmistakeable. Stacey's tender heart had seen her give away the bonus he'd paid to each member of the Party Planners team, and she'd done so quietly, without fanfare. This was the woman he'd allowed to slip through his fingers, and all for want of facing up to his past.

CHAPTER SIXTEEN

'CONGRATULATIONS!' BEAMING WIDELY, the doctor leaned over the desk to shake Stacey's hand. 'You must feel reassured to be under the care of your local clinic. It's a shock to learn you're expecting a baby when you're far from home. Do you have anyone to support you?'

'Financially, I don't need it. Emotionally...?' She shrugged.

'It's a lot to take in at first, but I'm sure you'll get your head around it soon.'

Thanking the doctor, she left the room. As soon as she'd spoken to Lucas the mist would clear, she hoped. There was just one small problem. She had to find him first. Bolting wasn't the answer. She should have stayed to confront him, but she'd been so angry and hurt. Now she had no excuse.

There was only one foolproof way to track him down.

'Niahl? How am I supposed to get in touch with Lucas when he won't pick up his phone?'

'You too,' Niahl commented.

'What do you mean, me too?'

'I imagine Luc is in the air by now.'

'You've spoken to him?'

'You left without saying goodbye. What's that about?'

'Do I cross-examine you?'

'All the time.'

'Not this time, Niahl,' she warned in a tone that told her brother she meant it.

'Because this time it's serious?'

'You took the words right out of my mouth. I heard you talking to him.'

'You mean you *overheard* us talking about you?' Niahl corrected her. 'What have I told you about that?'

'No lectures, Niahl. I need to speak to him.'

'How much of our conversation did you hear?'

'Enough,' she insisted.

'So you heard the part about him loving you like no other woman in his life before?'

'What?' she said faintly. 'I heard him say he overstepped, and that getting together with me was a huge error of judgement on his part. How does that square up with him loving me?'

'Simple. It takes time for any normal person to come to terms with the depth of their feelings, and you and Luc are far from normal. He's damaged and you're crazy impulsive sometimes.'

'Damaged?'

'Give him a chance to explain.'

There was a long pause, and then she asked, 'So you're okay with this?'

'Does it matter?'

'Of course it matters. Who else do I have to confide in?'

'Luc,' he suggested. 'That's if either of you can open up enough to trust each other with the truth.'

When the line was cut she stared blindly ahead, hollowed out at the thought that if Luc's barricades were high, hers were even higher, to the point where he'd found it easier to confide in her brother.

Even taking the pilot's seat, it seemed to take longer to fly to London than it ever had. He'd never been so restless or felt in such danger of losing something so vital to his life. He had to get this right. He'd tried to stay away from Stacey to save her from him, and had failed spectacularly. He'd made to love to her, yet never once told her how he felt. *Was it too late now?* They shared equally in their love for an unborn child, so it had to be possible to save the situation.

He *would* save the situation.

He *must*.

'Luc!' She shot up from her office desk so fast, he worried for her safety and crossed the room in a couple of strides. Whatever had gone before, his relief at seeing Stacey was so overwhelming he dragged her into his arms and kissed her over and over again.

'I was just ringing you,' she gasped when he let her up for air. 'I wanted to say that I'm so sorry I left without speaking to you. I acted on the spur of the moment, thinking I'd heard something when I hadn't, and—'

'Don't worry about that now,' he soothed. 'I should have answered my phone but I didn't, because all I could think of was seeing you again. I flew straight here, then drove from the airport.'

'You didn't need to worry. I got an appointment with the doctor the moment I got back. The baby's fine. I'm fine.'

'And now I'm fine too,' he confirmed with a slanting grin as he echoed Stacey's familiar mantra. Though, that wasn't quite true.

'Luc?' She knew at once that he was holding something back. 'What aren't you telling me?'

Relaxing his grip, he stepped back and admitted, 'There is something I have to tell you, but not here. My house?'

'You have a house in London?'

'Not too far away,' he confirmed. 'My car's right outside. Can you come now?'

She searched his eyes and must have seen the urgency in them. 'Of course. I'll ask my secretary to clear my diary, and then I'm all yours.'

Luc's London house was amazing. It was one of those smart white town houses in an elegant Georgian square with a beautifully manicured garden for the exclusive use of residents at its heart. The interior was exquisite, but soulless, Stacey decided until Luc led the way into a library that smelled of old books and leather.

'This is lovely.' She gasped as she turned full circle to take it in. The walls appeared to be composed entirely of books, and there were several inviting armchairs, as well as a welcoming fire behind a padded brass fender.

'I chose each of these books myself,' Luc explained as he followed her interested gaze. 'I can't claim credit for the rest of the house. Apart from the tech, it was designed by a team.'

'We rely a lot on teams, you and I,' she observed with a crooked smile. 'I suppose that's how we keep ourselves isolated so successfully. There's always a buffer between us and the world, and that's the way we like it.'

'That's the way I used to like it,' Luc admitted.

'And now?'

'And now I want to tell you why I am as I am, and why I've never told you that I love you.'

She was so shocked by Luc's declaration she couldn't find a single word to say. As the old clock on the mantelpiece ticked away the seconds they stared at each other with so much in their eyes it would have taken a week to express it, anyway.

Taking both her hands in his, Luc led her to the window where light was shining in. 'I closed off my heart…to you…to everything. It was the only way I could come to terms with the love I destroyed.'

Stacey's heart lurched, but she didn't dare to interrupt. Luc was staring out of the window looking as fierce as she'd ever seen him. 'I must have told you about my parents?' He shot her a look of sheer agony.

'Niahl spoke of them with great affection…' She couldn't remember Luc mentioning them once. In fact, if the subject of mothers and fathers ever came up, however innocent the reference, Luc would always clam up.

'Yes…yes, Niahl met them,' he confirmed, frowning as he no doubt examined the memory. 'Perhaps he told you they were eccentric—reckless, even—always coming up with new ideas?'

'Not really. He said they were funny and warm, and that they adored you and your brothers and sister, and that, unlike the farm, your family house was a real home.'

'He didn't mention they were practically penniless?'

'No.' She shook her head decisively. 'He said they were the most generous people he'd ever known, and that he loved visiting, because they always made him so welcome. I remember him saying that everything was so relaxed and friendly.' And now it was time for the hard question. 'So what went wrong?'

'Their death was my fault.'

Luc rattled off the words as if they had to be said but he couldn't bear to say them.

'How was it your fault?' Stacey pressed. 'They were killed in an air crash, weren't they? You weren't the pilot. You can't blame yourself for that.' Oh, yes, he could, she saw from Luc's expression.

'I'd just started to make some real money,' he said grimly, staring blindly out of the window. 'I was still working from my bedroom, but I was selling programs hand over fist. My parents had this new idea to make mobile buildings, of all things—it made perfect sense to them. My mother would design these portable homes, and my father would build them.'

'Niahl told me they were wonderful and so clever that he was always learning something from them, but I didn't realise they had those skills.'

'They didn't, and I told them so. They begged me to give them the chance to visit a factory a short flight away. I said of course, and gave them the money to book a ticket. I should have checked…'

'What should you have checked?' But Luc wasn't listening.

'How could I deny them when I had enough money to pay for the flight?' he murmured, narrowing his eyes as he thought back. 'I pointed out the difficulties they might encounter with this new business venture—the cash-flow problems, the complexities of hiring staff. The one thing I didn't think to insist on was that I booked the tickets, and so they went to a friend instead who'd built his own single-engine aircraft in the garage, and was always bragging about it, though he hadn't flown it for months—maybe never, for all I know. I guess my parents thought they could save me some money. They were never greedy. They didn't know what greed was, but they were…impressionable'

'Oh, Luc. You can't blame yourself for any of this.' He couldn't cry, either, Stacey realised. Luc was a man of iron, who ran a global enterprise that kept thousands of people in work, with brothers and a sister to whom he'd devoted a great part of his life. He'd had no time to grieve, and so he bottled it up, and when the anger became too great, he worked it off with physical exercise—polo, sex—anything would do, but as yet he'd found nothing to wipe out that pain.

He sighed. 'They just wanted a chance and I gave it to them. I killed them as surely as if I had been flying the plane.'

'No, you didn't,' she cut in fiercely. 'Their friend killed them and himself with his vanity. You're not to blame, any more than the child I used to be was to blame for my father's coldness towards me. My father suffered grief at the loss of my mother that he had no idea how to deal with. Don't be the same as him. Don't be like that with our child. Accept the pain and live with it, if you must, but promise me you'll never visit your suffering on our child.'

'*My* suffering?' Luc murmured, frowning.

'Yes. Your suffering, and the sooner you accept that and let me in, the sooner we can start to heal each other.'

There was silence for quite a time and then he said, 'When did you become so wise?'

She gave him a crooked smile. 'When I broke free of you and my brother?'

Luc laughed. He really laughed. Throwing back his head, he laughed until tears came to his eyes, and then she held him as he sobbed.

CHAPTER SEVENTEEN

A WEEK LATER Luc asked her to marry him.

'I can't think of anyone who'd be a better mother,' he mused as they lay in the bed they'd barely left for seven days. 'I love you, Stacey Winner. I should have told you years ago, but we are where we are.'

'And it's not too late to make amends,' she suggested.

'I was hoping you'd say that,' Luc agreed, turning his head lazily on the pillow so they could hold each other's gaze.

'I'd better marry you because I love you, and I can't think of anyone else who'd have you.'

'Or who'd put up with you,' he countered, smiling against her mouth.

'I just worry that there are dozens of women in the world better suited to your sophisticated life.'

'So change my life,' Luc insisted. 'Keep your job. Work. I'll never stop you. Whatever you want to do is fine by me, because that's who you are, the person I fell in love with, and I love you without reservation. I don't want a puppet I can bend to my will.

I love the challenge of you being you, in case you hadn't noticed?'

'I might have done,' Stacey admitted with a grin as they paused the conversation for a kiss...several kisses, as it turned out.

More kisses later, Luc added, 'I love complex, vibrant, capable you, and the last thing I want is to change you. That would be defeating the object, don't you think? Having rediscovered the only woman I could ever love as completely as I love you, I've realised there's more to life than work and money, and that this is the man I want to be...the man I am with you.'

'Marry me,' she whispered. 'I love you so much.'

'I will,' Luc promised solemnly.

'When?'

'Now! Today!' he enthused, shooting up in bed.

'Special licence?' she suggested.

'You're the expert,' he said with a burst of sheer happiness.

'But I doubt it can be today. As soon as possible?'

'Sounds good to me,' Luc confirmed, drawing her back into his arms.

'You want to get married right away because of the baby,' Stacey reasoned out loud.

They still had a way to go, Luc realised. Stacey had set him free, and now it was his turn to heal her, and if that took the rest of his life it was fine by him. 'Because of you,' he stated firmly. 'I can't let you get away a second time.'

'Really?' Her eyes widened on the most important question she'd ever ask.

'Really,' he confirmed, and then he kissed her as a future full of love, care, happiness and laughter finally came within their reach.

'Trust me, love me,' he whispered. 'I need you more than you know.'

EPILOGUE

THEY WERE CALLING it the wedding of the year. True to
her pledge, Stacey had arranged everything in record
time, so a mere six weeks after Luc's proposal here
they were, about to wear each other's ring.

Her wedding day was the culmination of almost an
entire lifetime of love for one man. There was nothing
imaginary about the splendour of the setting, or the
man waiting for her at the altar. The scent of countless pink and white blossoms filled the air, and the
abbey was full of her favourite people—notably her
brother, her team, and Lady Sarah, who had thankfully recovered in time to be her matron of honour.

The organ thundered and the voices of the choir
rose in heavenly chorus as she walked forward with
confidence into the next chapter of her life.

The pews were filled with the great and the good,
as well as her friends and Luc's polo team. There was
even a sprinkling of royalty. Lucas Da Silva was still
a Spanish grandee, after all. Her brother was giving
her away, and she had to say Niahl did look stunning in an impeccably tailored dark suit. He'd even

finger-combed his hair for the occasion, so it almost made him look less of a devil in a custom-made suit—though not quite…a fact that wasn't lost on the female members of the congregation, she noticed.

'Thank you for doing this,' she whispered as she attempted to glide alongside Niahl's giant footsteps.

'Don't thank me,' he whispered back, mischief brightening his sparkling green eyes. 'I thought I'd never get rid of you.'

'And now?'

'And now I couldn't be happier for you—or for Luc. You deserve each other.'

She hummed. 'Just when I thought you were being nice.'

'I was being nice,' Niahl insisted with a wicked grin as he stepped back to allow the ceremony to begin.

Lady Sarah, who was dressed beautifully for the occasion in a long, plain gown of soft lilac chiffon with a pink blush corsage of fresh flowers on her shoulder, took charge of Stacey's bouquet, and when Stacey whispered her thanks, she smiled.

'I think of you as the daughter I never had,' Lady Sarah had said as they got ready. 'There's no one I trust more than you, Stacey.' And then she'd cupped Stacey's cheek to elicit a promise. 'But I'll only do this for you on one condition. Now I'm back at the helm I expect you and Lucas to make the most of your lives, and not to spend all your time working.'

Lucas had come to the same conclusion, he told Stacey when she confided this to him. 'We're going to enjoy life together,' he'd stated, 'and I'm going to spoil you as you deserve to be spoiled. So if you receive a shipment from Paris, or a delivery from one of the foremost jewellers in the world, you'll just have to be brave.'

'I'll grit it out,' she'd promised, trying not to laugh.

This was a new chapter, and an entirely different life, as it would be for anyone who wasn't a billionaire, or a member of the aristocracy. But all that mattered to Stacey was that this was the start of a new life of love, which she would spend with a man she trusted with all her heart. Lucas would be at her side, as she would be at his, organising the heck out of him, as he'd put it.

When he took her hand in his, she wanted nothing more than to melt into him, kiss him, and be one with him, and that was before the ceremony had even begun.

'Patience,' he murmured, reading her as he always had.

That wouldn't be easy, she accepted as the voices of the choir rose in a sublime anthem. Somehow Lucas had managed to look more devastating than ever today, in an austere black suit with his crimson sash of office pinned with a jewel on his chest.

'And don't forget, I have a very special present for you,' he added discreetly.

What could that be? Surely not another piece of jewellery? Lucas had given her so much already, and had refused to take it back when she'd said the jewellery box he'd given her, laden to the brim with precious gems, was far in excess of anything she could ever need. Could it be another dress? She glanced down at the fabulous couture gown he'd insisted on having made for her in Paris. The slim sheath of silk to accommodate the first hint that she was pregnant had a discreet slit at one side. 'For ease of movement,' he'd said.

So he can whip it off fast, she thought.

But it was a beautiful gown. Encrusted with crystals and pearl, it boasted a cathedral-length train in silk chiffon that floated around her as she walked.

As they stood beneath the stained-glass windows, she couldn't help but feel the echo of countless other couples who had brought their hopes and dreams to this place and turned them into reality. 'I love you,' she whispered as Luc put the circle of diamonds on her wedding finger.

'And I love you more,' he said.

Finally the ceremony was over and they were showered with rose petals as they left the fragrant interior of the abbey for the sunshine and fresh air of a happy new day. She looked for the limousine she'd booked. 'But I organised a car,' she exclaimed worriedly.

'Of course you did,' Luc said, smiling. 'But I arranged a different sort of transport for the love of my life.'

She followed his dangerous black stare to where two horses, plaited up and dressed in their finest regalia, were being brought up to the foot of the steps. 'Ludo?' she breathed. 'Is that really Ludo?' She gazed up at Luc.

'Are you pleased?'

'Pleased? I've never been so happy to have an arrangement go wrong!'

'I thought you wouldn't mind riding to our wedding breakfast if you two were reunited,' Luc said as he helped her into the saddle. 'You might have to hitch up your dress…'

'I might have to do a lot of things to get used to this new life with you.' Dipping down from the saddle, she took Luc's face between her hands and kissed him. 'Thank you.'

'Thank *you*,' he said, turning serious. 'You gave me my life back and now I'm going to do the same for you.'

* * * * *

If you enjoyed
Snowbound with His Forbidden Innocent
*you're sure to enjoy these other stories
by Susan Stephens!*

The Sheikh's Shock Child
Pregnant by the Desert King
A Scandalous Midnight in Madrid
The Greek's Virgin Temptation

Available now!

WE HOPE YOU ENJOYED THIS BOOK!

HARLEQUIN

Presents®

Get lost in a world of international luxury, where billionaires and royals are sure to satisfy your every fantasy.

Discover eight new books every month, available wherever books are sold!

Harlequin.com

HPHALO2019

AVAILABLE THIS MONTH FROM
Harlequin Presents®

THE GREEK'S SURPRISE CHRISTMAS BRIDE
Conveniently Wed! • by Lynne Graham

THE QUEEN'S BABY SCANDAL
One Night with Consequences • by Maisey Yates

PROOF OF THEIR ONE-NIGHT PASSION
Secret Heirs of Billionaires • by Louise Fuller

SECRET PRINCE'S CHRISTMAS SEDUCTION
by Carol Marinelli

A DEAL TO CARRY THE ITALIAN'S HEIR
The Scandalous Brunetti Brothers • by Tara Pammi

CHRISTMAS CONTRACT FOR HIS CINDERELLA
by Jane Porter

SNOWBOUND WITH HIS FORBIDDEN INNOCENT
by Susan Stephens

MAID FOR THE UNTAMED BILLIONAIRE
Housekeeper Brides for Billionaires
by Miranda Lee

LOOK FOR THESE AND OTHER HARLEQUIN PRESENTS® BOOKS
WHEREVER BOOKS ARE SOLD, INCLUDING MOST BOOKSTORES,
SUPERMARKETS, DISCOUNT STORES AND DRUGSTORES.

HPATMBPA1219

COMING NEXT MONTH FROM

HARLEQUIN

Presents®

Available December 17, 2019

#3777 THE ITALIAN'S UNEXPECTED BABY
Secret Heirs of Billionaires
by Kate Hewitt
Mia is wary of trusting others, so when Alessandro coolly dismisses her after their night together, she dares not tell him she's pregnant! But on learning her secret, he's *determined* to legitimize his child...

#3778 SECRETS OF HIS FORBIDDEN CINDERELLA
One Night With Consequences
by Caitlin Crews
Overwhelming. Irresistible. Off-limits. Teo was all those things to Amelia. Until she attends his luxurious masquerade ball, and they share a deliciously anonymous encounter! Now Amelia must tell brooding Teo he's the father of her unborn baby...

#3779 CROWNING HIS CONVENIENT PRINCESS
Once Upon a Seduction...
by Maisey Yates
Nothing surprises Prince Gunnar, until personal assistant Latika asks him for help—by marrying her! Recognizing her desperation, he protects her with his royal name. Yet the biggest surprise isn't their sizzling chemistry, but how dangerously *permanent* his craving for Latika feels...

#3780 CLAIMED FOR THE DESERT PRINCE'S HEIR
by Heidi Rice
When Kasia comes face-to-face with Prince Raif at a lavish party, he looks furious—and dangerously sexy. For Kasia can't hide the truth...after their desert encounter, she's pregnant. And this time Raif won't let her go!

HPCNMRA1219

#3781 BILLIONAIRE'S WIFE ON PAPER
Conveniently Wed!
by Melanie Milburne

Logan can't lose his family estate. But to rescue it, he must wed! He avoids real relationships, having failed at love before. So when housemaid Layla suggests he take a convenient wife, he's intrigued...and proposes to her!

#3782 REDEEMED BY HIS STOLEN BRIDE
Rival Spanish Brothers
by Abby Green

Having stolen his rival's fiancée, billionaire Gabriel is blindsided by his powerful attraction to innocent Leonora! He believes he can offer her only passion, but Leonora knows her proud husband could offer so much more than pleasure...

#3783 THEIR ROYAL WEDDING BARGAIN
by Michelle Conder

Princess Alexa's strategy was simple: avoid an unwanted union by finding a short-term fiancé. Notoriously untamable Prince Rafaele seems her safest bet...until the king demands they marry, for real!

#3784 A SHOCKING PROPOSAL IN SICILY
by Rachael Thomas

To save her penniless family, Kaliana needs a husband—urgently! So she shockingly proposes to billionaire Rafe. Yet Rafe has his own agenda—a marriage could secure his rightful inheritance, but only if it appears to be real!

YOU CAN FIND MORE INFORMATION ON UPCOMING HARLEQUIN® TITLES, FREE EXCERPTS AND MORE AT WWW.HARLEQUIN.COM.

HPCNMRB1219

Get 4 FREE REWARDS!

We'll send you 2 FREE Books plus <u>2</u> FREE Mystery Gifts.

Harlequin Presents® books feature a sensational and sophisticated world of international romance where sinfully tempting heroes ignite passion.

FREE
Value Over
$20

YES! Please send me 2 FREE Harlequin Presents® novels and my 2 FREE gifts (gifts are worth about $10 retail). After receiving them, if I don't wish to receive any more books, I can return the shipping statement marked "cancel." If I don't cancel, I will receive 6 brand-new novels every month and be billed just $4.55 each for the regular-print edition or $5.80 each for the larger-print edition in the U.S., or $5.49 each for the regular-print edition or $5.99 each for the larger-print edition in Canada. That's a savings of at least 11% off the cover price! It's quite a bargain! Shipping and handling is just 50¢ per book in the U.S. and $1.25 per book in Canada.* I understand that accepting the 2 free books and gifts places me under no obligation to buy anything. I can always return a shipment and cancel at any time. The free books and gifts are mine to keep no matter what I decide.

Choose one: ☐ **Harlequin Presents®**
Regular-Print
(106/306 HDN GNWY)

☐ **Harlequin Presents®**
Larger-Print
(176/376 HDN GNWY)

Name (please print)

Address   Apt. #

City   State/Province   Zip/Postal Code

Mail to the **Reader Service:**
IN U.S.A.: P.O. Box 1341, Buffalo, NY 14240-8531
IN CANADA: P.O. Box 603, Fort Erie, Ontario L2A 5X3

Want to try 2 free books from another series? Call 1-800-873-8635 or visit www.ReaderService.com.

---

*Terms and prices subject to change without notice. Prices do not include sales taxes, which will be charged (if applicable) based on your state or country of residence. Canadian residents will be charged applicable taxes. Offer not valid in Quebec. This offer is limited to one order per household. Books received may not be as shown. Not valid for current subscribers to Harlequin Presents books. All orders subject to approval. Credit or debit balances in a customer's account(s) may be offset by any other outstanding balance owed by or to the customer. Please allow 4 to 6 weeks for delivery. Offer available while quantities last.

Your Privacy—The Reader Service is committed to protecting your privacy. Our Privacy Policy is available online at www.ReaderService.com or upon request from the Reader Service. We make a portion of our mailing list available to reputable third parties that offer products we believe may interest you. If you prefer that we not exchange your name with third parties, or if you wish to clarify or modify your communication preferences, please visit us at www.ReaderService.com/consumerschoice or write to us at Reader Service Preference Service, P.O. Box 9062, Buffalo, NY 14240-9062. Include your complete name and address.

HP20

SPECIAL EXCERPT FROM

HARLEQUIN

Presents®

*Layla never imagined Logan would choose her!
She feels far from the perfect bride. Yet to protect her
home, she'll wear Logan's ring... But can she ignore
the burning connection threatening to destroy their
temporary arrangement?*

*Read on for a sneak preview of Melanie Milburne's
next story for Harlequin Presents,*
Billionaire's Wife on Paper.

"But you don't want to get married." It was a statement, not a question.

A shadow passed through his gaze like a background figure moving across a stage. He turned back to face the view from the windows; there might as well have been a keep-away sign printed on his back. It seemed a decade before he spoke. "No." His tone had a note of finality that made something in Layla's chest tighten.

The thought of him marrying someone one day had always niggled at her like a mild toothache. She could ignore it mostly, but now and again a sharp jab would catch her off guard. But how could he ever find someone as perfect for him as Susannah? No wonder he was a little reluctant to date seriously these days. If only Layla could find someone to love her with such lasting loyalty. Sigh.

"What about a marriage of convenience? You could find someone who would agree to marry you just long enough to fulfill the terms of the will."

One of his dark eyebrows rose in a cynical arc above his left eye. "Are you volunteering for the role as my paper bride?"

Eek! Why had she even mentioned such a thing? Maybe it was time to stop reading paperback romances and start reading thriller or horror novels instead. Layla could feel a hot flush of color flooding her cheeks and bent down to straighten the items in her basket to disguise it. "No. Of course not." Her voice was part laugh, part gasp, and came out shamefully high and tight. Her? His bride of convenience?

Ha-di-ha-ha-ha. She wouldn't be a convenient bride for anyone, much less Logan McLaughlin.

A strange silence crept from the far corners of the room, stealing oxygen particles, stilling dust motes, stirring possibilities…

Logan walked back to where she was hovering over her cleaning basket, his footsteps steady and sure. Step. Step. Step. Step. Layla slowly raised her gaze to his inscrutable one, her heart doing a crazy tap dance in her chest. She drank in the landscape of his face—the prominent ink-black eyebrows over impossibly blue eyes, the patrician nose, the sensually sculpted mouth, the steely determined jaw. The lines of grief etched into his skin that made him seem older than he was. At thirty-three, he was in the prime of his life. Wealthy, talented, a world-renowned landscape architect—you could not find a more eligible bachelor…or one so determined to avoid commitment.

"Think about it, Layla."

His tone was deep with a side note of roughness that made a faint shiver course through her body. A shiver of awareness. A shiver of longing that could no longer be restrained in its secret home.

Layla picked up her basket from the floor and held it in front of her body like a shield. Was he teasing her? Making fun of her? He must surely know she wasn't marriage material—certainly not for someone like him. She was about as far away from Susannah as you could get. "Don't be ridiculous."

His hand came down to touch her on the forearm, and even through two layers of clothing her skin tingled. She looked down at his long strong fingers and disguised a swallow. She could count on one hand the number of times he had touched her over the years and still have fingers left over. His touch was unfamiliar and strange, alien almost, and yet her body reacted like a crocus bulb to spring sunshine.

"I'm serious," he said, looking at her with watchful intensity. "I need a temporary wife to save Bellbrae from being sold or destroyed, and who better than someone who loves this place as much as I do?"

Don't miss
Billionaire's Wife on Paper.
*Available January 2020 wherever Harlequin Presents®
books and ebooks are sold.*

Harlequin.com

Copyright © 2019 by Melanie Milburne

HPEXP1219R

Coming next month,
Surrender to this tale of sinful seduction…

Overwhelming. Irresistible. Off-limits. Teo de Luz was all those things to innocent Amelia. Until she attends his opulent masquerade ball, and they share a deliciously anonymous encounter! Now Amelia must tell this brooding Spaniard he's the father of her unborn child.

Teo can't forget his runaway Cinderella, but discovering her true identity stuns him. His loathing of Amelia's family means he cannot dismiss her deception! He will marry her. He will claim his heir. And he'll exact a sensual revenge on Amelia, one pleasurable night at a time…

Secrets of His Forbidden Cinderella

Available January 2020

HPBPA1219R